MARKED BY DRAGON'S BLOOD

RETURN OF THE DRAGONBORN BOOK 1

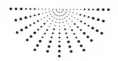

N.M. HOWELL

Written in collaboration with

H.F. STARK

Cover by

COVERS BY JUAN

DUNGEON MEDIA CORP.

To anyone who has ever been bullied, judged, persecuted, or forgotten because of who they are or where they come from.
The world is more beautiful because you are in it.

PROLOGUE

HIGHTOWYR. IT WAS ONCE THE GREATEST CITY IN THE western-most reaches of the province of Noelle, in the great land of Shaeyara, and was ruled by a powerful royal lineage. The streets of that ancient city were bursting with sorcerers and sorceresses, all dedicating their lives and resources to innovation, knowledge, and the perpetual ascension of magical might. But the city fell. And almost all of the great magical minds who survived, fled to the far side of the continent. That magnificent royal lineage became a byword and a whisper. For centuries, the city languished in ruin and darkness.

As the land lay wasted and devastated, collapsing on itself, the rest of Noelle flourished. Great cities like Taline to the north and Thabes in the True Isles, rose up from the earth and became beacons of knowledge, power, and beauty. Eventually, the few sorcerers who had remained in Hightowyr grew jealous and angry. In the five hundred years they had managed to stay alive in the ruins of the city, only that envy and hatred was powerful enough to cause them to shed their weariness. They began searching for ways to bring the people back, to encourage the greatest magical beings to return to the city and help rebuild, but the sins and the destruction of the past had not been forgotten. No one would come.

Riddled by their own failure and their endless rage, these seven men and women made a pact and a sacrifice. They each tasked their families to build a university; for these seven had been among the most brilliant of that lost time and had passed all their knowledge to their families. It was meant to be the greatest university in Noelle. No matter what happened, regardless of forces acting upon the city or time ravaging the earth, their descendants were to watch over that institution and seek, above all, to be the most prestigious and powerful.

As for the seven themselves, they vowed to use every ounce of their considerable magic to rebuild as much of the city as they could. And for one year, they did. For one year, they worked tirelessly to clear the rubble and strengthen the foundation. For one year, they touched the ground, drawing the stains of dark magic from the earth. For one year, they pulled on every bit of magic in their bodies, even the core spirit centers of their souls. But it was too much. By the end of the year, they each fell sick and, shortly after, wasted away.

True to their word, their families established the University. They created it in the gargantuan black marble husk of the ancient mint and the many annexes once used by the royal government. They began to invite new students. At first, only the poor came, as the wealthy and the truly brilliant went to the beautiful, inveterate universities across Noelle. But as the years passed and word spread of the potential of the Hightowyr University, more people came. Hundreds. Then thousands. The University gained wealth, prestige, and professors who were known the world over. The time came when the past was too distant to have its name in the present, and so the city and the University were renamed.

Arvall City began.

Today, one thousand years after the fall of Hightowyr, Arvall City is the greatest urban center in all of Noelle. Perhaps even in all of Shaeyara. Taline is the closest rival, but that wonderful city has been plagued by terrorist attacks for thirteen years. Arvall City built itself on the ruins of Hightowyr, its infrastructure rising in tandem with the ruins in some places and covering the old stone completely in others. While Hightowyr was stone and mortar, Arvall City is made of glass and steel, its buildings rising hundreds of feet in the air and catching the sun to make it a city of light and promise and might. At the south end of the city, the buildings have been built right into the mountainside. The mountain is Brie, and even after its hard trials and the Great Erosion of the Third Cycle, it is still the tallest mountain in the world. No one knows for sure how tall it is, but its peak pierces the atmosphere, and soars even taller still.

The University sits high upon the mountainside, even higher than the buildings, and sprawls across the vast bowl that was made in the mountain in a time before memory. From the other side of the city, the University looks like some great, dark specter, menacing Arvall from its perch. Bordering the city to the east is the beginning of the String Fields, and to the west is the Spider Sea. To the north are a smattering of small towns and hamlets, one of which is Michaelson, where a powerful sorceress named Andie was riding the train, heading to Arvall City.

It was the two hundred eleventh day of the Ninth Cycle of the First Age. So it began.

CHAPTER ONE

SHE WAS FLYING. NO, NOT JUST FLYING, BUT SOARING high above the gold and rolling fields of Michaelson. Not too slow or too fast, but at that perfect speed that allowed her to feel exhilarated, while still giving her the presence of mind to see and feel and need her surroundings. Soon, she left Michaelson behind and was so high that she couldn't follow her shadow on the ground. The farther she was from home, the higher she flew until she was nearing the edge of Arvall City, and the clouds were nearing overhead.

She felt so good, so unlimited, that she thought her heart would burst as she soared in the soft, iridescent glow of the evening sun. There was no wind, no friction on her skin, and nothing whipping or rolling in the breeze. And even though she knew this was odd, she liked it: the feeling of flying and being still at the same time. It felt like she belonged.

She was only just nearing Brie when she was swallowed by darkness. Then there was no wind, no light, no sound, no sensation, or movement at all. There was only a nameless, formless pain—an anguish so vast and terrible that it wasn't just in the darkness. It was the darkness. She couldn't tell if it was coming from some other source or from herself, but it was crushing. Maddening. But then she heard it. It was even worse than the anguish. Screaming.

"MA'AM?"

Andie woke with a jolt, her books slipping from her lap. She turned toward the voice and saw a stewardess.

"Ma'am, are you okay? Bad dream?"

"I'm... I'm fine. Yeah, bad dream. I'm sorry, was I too loud?"

"No, not at all," the stewardess said, suddenly smiling. "You never made a sound. It's just that ... Well, the spellglass."

She pointed toward the window and Andie followed her finger. Spellglass looked like regular glass, yet anyone with magic in their blood could control its shape and density with only a thought. The spellglass had totally transformed, becoming opaque and protruding like knife points in some places, while in others, it flowed like liquid. It was like a tesseract that could *feel*, that kept collapsing on itself and rebuilding in the same instant. With just one thought, Andie calmed the spellglass. It returned to its normal state.

"Is there anything I can get for you, ma'am?"

"No, I'm fine," Andie said, embarrassed and not wanting to seem like a charity case. "I'll try to stay awake."

The stewardess smiled and walked away. Andie took a deep breath and looked out the window. Most of her life was passing her by: the mayor's fields, the coal mine, the Forest of the Orange Pines where the poorest farmers lived, and the little twin creeks snaking their wet bodies through the fields with impunity. She had lived in Michaelson her entire life, and though she had been in Arvall City almost regularly since she and her father stopped going into Taline years ago, it still felt as if she was doing something adventurous and new.

She bent forward to pick up her books, still shaken by that beautiful and terrible dream. All of them were there; everything she needed for her first semester of classes at the University. But there was one she couldn't find. It wasn't for school, and in fact, she shouldn't have even been reading it on the train. She was never supposed to take it from the house, let alone be seen with it in public. As she told herself to stay calm, she started to panic anyway. She tried not to think of what her father would say if she had lost it. He'd be furious, or worse—disappointed. Suddenly, a blonde head peeped around the seat in front of her.

"Lose something?"

"Oh, yeah." Andie forced a small smile. "I'm sorry, I didn't mean to disturb you. It's just that I lost one of my books and I thought it might have slid under your seat."

"I think you mean... this!" the girl exclaimed, flourishing the book like the end of some corny magician's routine. She clearly didn't care if anyone saw the title of the book. From Dragons to Men.

"Oh... Uh..." Andie fumbled, anxious and baffled.

"This is pretty heavy. Someone has a lot to say about... er... dragons and men. Ooh, sounds exciting! Here."

She handed the book to Andie as if it were just a thing, maybe a leaflet from the Church of Stone and Sea. Andie took it, thanked the girl, and quickly tucked the book away into the bottom of her bag, where she planned to keep it safely hidden from prying eyes until she was locked away in her new apartment. She gave the girl another smile and then gazed out of the window, turning the spellglass into a double-paned latticework that transformed the early morning light as it streamed in the train compartment. The girl was still peeping around the chair, eyeing her curiously. Andie felt uneasy, but she didn't want to be rude so she did her best to smile back and then turned her attention back towards the window. She wasn't in the mood for talking and definitely didn't want to encourage the very thing the girl did next.

The trains in Noelle were golden, sleek, and narrow. The seats were arranged in single file, with a moderate walkway running parallel. If someone wanted to talk to a friend behind them, they'd have to press a button to swivel the chair around, which is exactly what the blonde girl did, nearly tripping a steward in the process.

"Oh, no! I'm so sorry. I'm such a cub sometimes. So," she said, turning her attention to Andie, oblivious. "I'm Tristtle."

"Andryne," Andie said as she extended her hand. Her eyes then widened and she quickly corrected, "I mean, Andie. Please." She extending her hand, hoping the girl wouldn't latch on to her real name. She cursed herself for letting it slip. She didn't even know why it had slipped from her lips, as she hadn't gone by that name since her mother had died. No one outside her family knew her by that name. The girl beamed back at her.

"Wow, super old-fashioned. Andie. So cute. Totally blue. I didn't know people still shook hands. I'm not a germaphobe or stranger-phobic, or even phobic at all, but it's really... vintage. Blue, you know? Anyway, so I'm totally on my way to see my uncle. He's a total boss. I'm going to see him *eternally* and I'm not sure why, because I don't really like him, but I'm here like flow. Between us girls, it's really his money I'm after. I'm not a bum or anything—and I'm completely not bum-phobic—but he's got money on top of money. I should probably keep things like that to myself. I'm such a cub. But he's this really big architect who designs all kinds of buildings and stuff, and now he's working on the tallest tower in Vall and he—"

"I'm sorry, where?" Andie said, not wanting the answer so much as a break for silence.

"Vall. Arvall City? They're saying this thing is going to be a monster, which is okay, I guess, even though I thought it was going to be a little baby business building—super cool, super blue..."

Andie had her mother's unfailing kindness, and so she listened to Tristtle talk and even made a genuine effort to focus on the conversation. Yet her mind wandered to Arvall City and all the things waiting for her there. Towers that touched the sky, standing closer together than dogs in the field. Strange powered vehicles floating through the city in dense, angry waves, with the mist from their crystals trailing in soft pastel clouds. Trains that ran vertical, up the sides of buildings. Red Ravens, which had been given civil liberties in Arvall City, just as they had been in Taline. And, of course, the Academy. She'd seen all these things before, but never as a student. Never as someone who belonged there.

The Academy was the department of the University

that instructed students in their first year. It was the second most rigorous year of the program—the most demanding being the last year. First year students went to classes year-round, with only ten breaks of ten days each. That meant that for three hundred of the four hundred days of the year, Andie would be in class. To her, it was as daunting as it was thrilling. She longed to learn, to discover, to grow. And, more than anything, she desired greater control over her dragon magic before it got her killed.

After almost an hour, the train finally pulled into the station.

"So, promise to look me up sometime?" Tristtle asked.

"I'd love to," Andie said, thinking that Tristtle was kind of sweet in her own way.

"Super blue. And I've totally been eyeing your books the whole ride. Are you going to the University?"

"Yeah. I start at the Academy today."

Tristtle was silent for a moment; Andie didn't think anything of it until Tristtle looked like she'd stopped breathing.

"Are you... still alive?" Andie asked.

"Yes. Yes!" Tristtle said, suddenly full of life. "I just can't believe I've been sitting here with a sorceress this whole time. Hey," she said, leaning closer. "Ever used your magic at home?"

"Of course not," Andie lied. "It's illegal unless you've graduated the University."

"Of course. I'm such a cub. Anyway, I hope I see you again soon."

When she was gone, Andie breathed a sigh of relief and packed up the rest of her books, making sure *Dragons* was on the bottom. She left the train and before long was heading down Avenue 204. The whole city was laid out in a perfect grid: numerical avenues running from north to south and magical herb names running from east to west. She was seeing the city through new eyes. The air here was thinner, cooler. In fact, Arvall itself was on the mountain, only much lower than the University. Truth be told, Brie started some one hundred kilometers before the incline became noticeable. The city was vast and Andie knew the avenues went up to at least one thousand.

She shook herself and tried to focus. She was a couple days later than she'd intended to be, but what had delayed her was unavoidable. For some time, she'd been caring for her father—his illness was part physical, but, more than anything, it was the result of a broken heart and crushed spirit. The tragedy that had hit their family had fractured him and he would never recover. Andie knew that.

Now that she was starting school, she had decided to hire a healer to live with him. It didn't feel right, and it wasn't what she wanted, but it was paramount that she learn to control her magic. Just days ago, the healer had disappeared, totally unreachable.

The woman Andie eventually hired was a nonagenarian, with her hair wrapped so tight it was a wonder it didn't cut off all circulation above the neck. Her voice was oddly musical and strident at the same time. She wasn't a great fit, but in all honesty, Andie didn't really trust anyone other than herself to take care of her father.

"It's only until I finish school," she thought out loud. "And then I'll be all his again."

Even so, the guilt was crushing her as she reached the financial district. Even necessity can't assuage guilt. Her father had wanted this even more than Andie did, and it was he who had convinced her to go. She breathed out a deep sigh as she slowly made her way down the winding street.

"You need to learn control," he'd said.

"Teach me. You used to be on the council. I know you can do it."

"That was the council in Taline, and you know how it ended. I don't want you anywhere near those people, but you need to be able to protect yourself. I can't risk someone catching us practicing here. And even if I wanted to..."

He didn't finish his sentence, but held up his hands as they trembled uncontrollably.

"Dad, I won't forgive myself for leaving you."

"Andie, this is for your life. Go. We'll find someone who can stay with me. You're my daughter. It should've been me taking care of you. Go."

HE WAS RIGHT. She'd already been putting off the Academy for years and if she did it again, she would lose her eligibility. More than that, it was time Andie began to live, truly live. She couldn't spend her entire life hiding behind her father and wanting her mother.

She boarded SKY 6 and thought of her past, present, and future as the train sped through the seemingly endless city. She watched as they passed hundreds of other trains going up and down and turning all over the city and its buildings. Up ahead was the University, claiming most of the mountain side and looming like the powerful and dangerous place it was. She loved that she'd gotten her magic from her mother, but sometimes she wished more than anything that she didn't have dragon blood or the powerful and unpredictable magic that came with it. Dragon blood had brought her family nothing but trouble.

The train reached the base of the next and steepest incline, and Andie watched the world from almost a ninety-degree angle as the train climbed the mountain side. It was a quick ride and she was soon standing on campus, taking a few deep breaths to acclimate herself to the atmosphere.

She'd only taken a few steps when she saw it. She didn't even know they still had these signs. There weren't even enough dragon blooded people left to warrant this kind of hate. It was unbelievable, but there it was: a sign with a young girl whose hands were softly glowing purple. There was a black crossed circle over her torso and it sent a clear, terrible message. Andie didn't know which was more disturbing: the sign's existence, the girl's age, or the fact that the sign looked brand new.

Just then, a man hurrying by bowled right into her and nearly knocked her down. He didn't apologize, never even stopped walking. Anger ripped through Andie. Her magic flared and the man tripped. He hit his head on the sign as he fell. Andie rushed to him.

"Are you okay?"

"Get off me!" he said, regaining his feet and hurrying off.

It wasn't exactly the welcome she'd hoped for.

LATER THAT EVENING, Andie was back down the mountain at city level. Her first day at the Academy hadn't really been a first day at all. The only thing she'd managed to do was miss both her classes—which were actually scheduled for two hours before she even got there—and find out that she still needed an icon. Icons were the size and shape of almonds and a prerequisite for study at the University. They monitored the students, made sure they stayed out of trouble and were safe. They were magical monitoring devices made of gold, bear wicker, and a proprietary blend of spells, and were essentially just a way for the University to spy on its students. Fortunately, her father had warned her about them before hand, so she wasn't surprised when they handed her hers.

The University once used bracelets with computer chips, but those were too easy to turn off. Andie had picked up an icon on the way down and now was searching for her apartment. She knew she was in the right part of town. University Park. It was where University students went who didn't have much money. There were other communities for students on scholarship and wealthy students. University Park was built over the ruins of Hightowyr, like the rest of the city, but this was the part of the city that got the least new infrastructure and the least maintenance. There were places here where the ancient ruins were still visible. Even now, Andie was passing what was left of an arch. First, they got to live in barely habitable apartments, then they got to deal with debt for the rest of their lives. She turned and, sure enough, could still see the black marble of the University sitting on the throne of the mountainside.

Even with the map she picked up at the University registrar's office, Andie still had a hard time finding her way. She'd never been this deep in the city before. It was a wonderful city to be lost in—beautiful, storied, massive, and diverse—but it was getting late. She turned a few more corners, just because, and found a dragon post.

Or what was left of it.

The University had had them all destroyed when the hate first started, leaving only the foundations as a warning and a threat. Dragon posts were where the dragons used to land to keep watch over the area. Legend said the dragon posts were huge, nearly half a kilometer high, and made of gold and iron. Dragons would land there and, with their keen eyes, spy across the land, keeping watch on all they knew and loved.

That was before the hate began. Before the dragons and the dragonborn people were betrayed and hunted to extinction.

Andie stopped and stared at the map. It wasn't possible for her to be this lost. She knew that this section of the city wasn't well taken care of and the streets here ran in every direction possible, rendering the grid completely useless, but she'd been walking for almost an hour. Two women were passing so she hurried over to ask directions.

"Excuse me," she said. "Could you point me to the corner of Rholdan and Avenue 652?"

"It's only ten blocks that way," the taller one said. "You can get there in fifteen minutes. That's an odd-looking map. May I?"

Andie handed her the map and it was only a moment before the women began to giggle.

"I'm sorry, dear, but this map is over a hundred and twenty years old. I can't imagine how it's still in this good of shape. See here..."

Andie followed the slim finger. In the lower left hand corner she saw the date: Two Hundredth Day of the Seventh Cycle of the First Age. The University was preparing to celebrate five hundred years and they were beginning to put out some of their old memorabilia. She must've picked from the wrong pile.

"Oh," she said. "I see."

"Well, goodbye. Remember, ten blocks that way."

The women left and Andie smacked herself in the head. One hundred and twenty years?

"Great job, Andie," she said to herself. "Maybe you need a lesson in how to tell time. A Life Age equals sixteen thousand years. An Age is two thousand years. A Cycle is one hundred twenty-five years. One year is four-hundred days. Do you think you can manage to read things before you take them from now on? Sorceresses don't live for hundreds of years anymore, so maybe you'd like to spend your time more wisely."

Still beating herself up, she headed in the direction the lady had pointed and in fifteen minutes she was staring up at her apartment building: a hole in the wall that looked as dingy and run down as the ethnic restaurant it sat on top of.

Climbing the stairs didn't inspire confidence, either, since they were so creaky the sound almost seemed to come before her foot fell. She met with her landlady, a middle-aged spinster who seemed to have given up on life entirely. She never spoke a word, simply handed Andie the keys and held up seven fingers to show her which floor to go to. She seemed incredibly ordinary, even if jaded, and Andie probably wouldn't have given Kristole another thought if she hadn't seen the mark on the back of her neck. A tattoo of a hand in flames. It stuck in Andie's mind as she climbed to the seventh floor and found her room. As she approached the door, she slowed. It was open and there were sounds inside. She paused, half wanting to go inside and half knowing she should get help. Yet, of the many things she was, a coward wasn't one of them. She crept to the door and opened it, her hand at the level of her eyes, ready for anything. She pushed the door open and saw a man in overalls. He turned at the sound of her entry.

"This ain't a robbery," he said. "I'm just fixing the window."

"Um. Okay. Can I have your name, sir?"

"I'm just the handyman. I work downstairs.

Speaking of which, they're expecting you. Better go down soon as you're settled."

"Yes. Right. 'They.' And what're you doing here again?"

"Window," he said, tapping the glass with his screwdriver.

"Of course," she muttered under her breath, cautiously crossing the living room as she kept an eye on him.

She set her things down in the kitchen, what little there was of it, and looked out of the window at her surprisingly spectacular view. She could see over the four blocks directly across from her building, all the way to an incredible complex of glass towers. It was the publishing district, which handled the magical, philosophical, business, and religious text for practically all of Noelle. Andie thought it was the coolest thing she'd seen yet.

After a couple minutes of gazing out into the night, she walked over to close the curtains, or, at least, the rags that were pretending to be curtains, and checked out her apartment. It was small, but she'd expected that. Aside from the shabby curtains, nothing looked bad at all. It was incredibly clean, had good proportions, new tiles, and everything in the bathroom and kitchen worked. She was especially thankful for the gas stove. Electrical ones frequently melted. She even had an ice maker in the fridge that was noisily busy at work. The kitchen faced the living room, divided from it only by a thin partition to which the counter was attached. The bathroom was the first door to the right in the hallway and, although it was clean, there was barely enough space to turn around. A small closet was across from it. Her bedroom was at the end of the hall— actually, twice as big as she'd expected—and her mattress and frame had already been delivered.

She decided to put a couple things out, just to start making it feel like home. She placed her books on the shelves of the small stand in the living room and set her mother's picture on top of it, but only for a moment before she decided to move it to her bedroom. Her mother had been beautiful, brunette, and powerful. Andie remembered that. She wasn't much older than Andie was when she died. Andie hid her small bag with *Dragons* in it under the bed. And then it was time to go downstairs and meet the mysterious "they."

She went downstairs to the restaurant, which had an alarming number of grills, and stood in a place where she could be seen by everybody. Hopefully "they" knew what she looked like because she couldn't identify them. It was only a moment before a man came up to her, smiling. He seemed middle-age, pushing the back end of the age group, and his face was covered in stubble. Yet, he didn't seem unkempt, just sweet and tired. He extended his hand.

"Hi. I'm Marvo," he said.

"Andie," she said, shaking hands with him. "I'm sorry, I don't mean to be rude, but—"

"But how do I know you? I knew your father many years ago. As a matter of fact, we met under similar circumstances. I met him the day he first started at the Academy."

"Wow, you're Marvo? *The* Marvo? My dad used to tell me stories about you. You guys were great friends."

"Yeah, it's a shame how people grow apart. And it's a travesty what happened to your father."

"Um... thank you," she said, turning a bit.

It wasn't a subject she liked to talk about, even with her father.

"Here, let's sit down," Marvo said.

He took her to a table in the corner and motioned for a server to come over.

"We'd like some cloudcakes, please. There should still be some batter left from the batch we made this afternoon. I assume your father told you about my cloudcakes," he said, turning back to Andie.

"He's told everyone. I think they're more famous in Michaelson than Arvall City itself. So, if you were at the Academy, are you a practicing sorcerer?"

"Oh, no, I was never at the Academy. I only mentioned it because your father was going there. I'm a non-magic person, or a nomag, as we call them in the city. My family's always been nomag and always married nomags. Not that we have anything against magic. In fact, we've always been friends of sorcerers and sorceresses, but the magic life was never for us."

"We have the same term in the country. So, what do you do?"

"I cook. You're sitting in my restaurant. I bet you've probably got some questions about how your father was back then. I know I've got some about how he is now. But it's your first night in Arvall, and I don't want you to spend it having your ear talked off by an old-timer. We'll have plenty of time to talk later. Welcome to the city."

"Thank you."

Marvo stood and after a final parting smile, he turned and went back to the kitchen. Andie sat, waiting for her food, wondering why she never figured out that Marvo was a nomag or why her father never told her. She looked around the unimpressive restaurant, noting its general dinginess and almost hidden antiquity. The place was old—judging by some of the fixtures and the design of the molding, *very* old—and Andie began to see that it wasn't that Marvo's family weren't good with maintaining or cleaning, only that time was finally catching up. While she was gazing around, and beginning to sense the charm of the old place, she saw a boy coming to her with a plate of cloudcakes. He was tall, black-haired, and muscled in a sinewy kind of way; clearly used to hard work. He was handsome, surprisingly so. He was smiling, seemingly at no one, as if it just felt good to smile, to be happy and excited about life. Even from a distance, Andie could tell he had a warm spirit. He set the cloudcakes down on her table.

"These are my dad's secret recipe, and I do mean *secret*. He'll let me go over his checkbook, but he won't tell me what's in these. I'm Raesh," he said, extending his hand as his father had done.

"Andie. So why so secretive? Do these cure Maeludrax disease or something?"

"No, but if you have Maeludrax, this might be the only thing that will take your mind off it. That is, unless you have a girl you can't take your eyes off."

"Oh."

That was all she could manage. Raesh was doing just that: not taking his eyes off her. His smile was warm and sweet, and she could tell that he was probably a good person, but his bravado had shocked her. Or was he just really friendly? As beautiful as she was, Andie didn't have much experience with boys in Michaelson. The boys still tended to go after girls who were less work and less picky. As all that was going through her mind, Raesh sat down across from her at the table and the surprise only deepened.

"So, go ahead," he said. "Try them."

Andie gave herself a little shake to move past the surprise, and then picked up her fork. The cloudcakes were at least a foot wide, each thick enough to be three regular cloudcakes, and there were four of them. There was no way she could eat them all. But they looked and smelled incredible. Raesh reached to hand her the syrup, or so she thought, until he began to pour it for her. She watched his hand roam slowly back and forth above the plate, his face totally at ease, as if nothing about pouring a stranger's syrup was unusual. Andie couldn't keep back the smirk that rose to her lips. This guy was bold.

"There. Waiting for you," he said.

Andie pushed the fork into the cloudcakes and it sank right through. She cut out a bite and ate. It was beyond words. Perfect.

"That's fantastic," she said. "The syrup, too. What is this?"

"I have no idea. The syrup is a secret, too. He comes in an hour earlier than everyone else and bars us from the kitchen until he's done making the batter. He mixes a giant barrel of the syrup on the weekends. Can you believe he carries all of his spices and the recipes in a briefcase, which he locks in a safe or keeps by his side?"

"That's some secret, but I have to say it's worth it. These are the best cloudcakes I've ever had. By far. And I've eaten a lot of cloudcakes. Perfect meal for a first night."

"So, you like cloudcakes? Add that to the list. I know your name, I know you're a first-year sorceress, and I know your eyes are incredible. Not a bad start I've made for myself."

"No one's going to accuse you of being shy," Andie said, grinning.

"I could be subtle, but then who'd be here to make you smile?"

Andie just grinned and nodded. She couldn't help it, he was magnetic.

"But, seriously, I hope you enjoyed your first day. I know the city's not the kindest place, especially not *this* city, so I hope it was on its best behavior."

"Well... no. But I guess it could've been worse. At least I finally made it here in one piece."

"Ah, got lost in University Park, huh? Don't feel bad, the streets in this part of the city can do some weird things. Trust me, you'll be weaving your way around like a native in no time. You must be excited to start at the Academy."

"Yeah. I think. It's a complicated thing with me."

"That only makes me want to know more, but I can take a hint. I've always wanted that. Magic. I guess it's just not for some people. My cousin got it though. She's in her second year."

"I thought your dad said your family was nomag?"

"Most of us are. My dad's side of the family is completely non-magic. No one ever married anyone with magic until he married my mother. Couldn't help himself, I guess. And even on my mother's side it's hit and miss. That side is like a lot of other families these days. You just never know who's gonna get magic and who won't since the bloodlines are so diluted and mixed. But my cousin on my mother's side was a hit. So, I know what's up. Just wish I hadn't been a miss. I guess moms aren't as quick to pass their genes down."

He was quiet for a few moments after that. Andie watched him and she could see the sadness there, but also the immense warmth. Even though he wasn't living the life he wanted, he was still living life. It was admirable. But what he'd said about mothers had struck home. She needed to move.

"I'll be right back," she said. "Which way is the restroom?"

"Right in that corner back there."

She moved quickly through the tables and through the swinging doors that led to the hallway where the men's restroom was on one side and the women's on the other. Inside the restroom, she locked the door and turned to the mirror. There they were, eyes and nose and mouth and cheeks and hair and the barely noticeable soft dusting of freckles. All passed right down from her mother as reminders. Andie could see in all the old pictures how much they looked alike. Looking in the mirror was like looking at the face of the woman who was getting harder to remember with each passing day. Andie turned from the mirror. She took off her jacket and rolled up her sleeve.

On the underside of her forearm, a pattern was emerging, slowly but surely, more and more palpable with every week. The pattern was in tiny heptagon shapes and now a few hundred were visible there. The skin still felt the same, though she suspected that would change, too, with time. The pattern had begun to turn iridescent, not quite shining, but mesmerizingly colorful. And it was as terrifying as it was beautiful.

She quickly pulled her sleeve down to cover the evidence that could easily have her killed. She held her hand firmly over her sleeve, wondering just what she was thinking, risking her life by moving to the most dangerous place in the world for her kind.

Raesh was wrong. Mothers could pass on genes just fine.

CHAPTER TWO

Raesh followed her up the stairs, bringing up a plate of extra food that he and his father insisted she have. It was unnecessary, of course, because she'd eaten so much of the cloudcakes in an effort to finish them that she didn't think she'd be hungry until this time the next night. He was still trying to change her mind.

"My dad meant what he said. You don't need to pay to live here. The room is yours. Take advantage of the hospitality."

"That's incredibly kind of both of you, but I can't do that. I insist on having a job around here, it doesn't matter what."

"Your dad sent you here because he knew my dad would be able to help you."

"You're probably right," she said, stopping and turning to face him. "But my dad should've told me who he was sending me to, that way I could have insisted Marvo give me a job before I even came in to settle down. Besides, the landlady didn't seem like she'd be okay with anyone freeloading."

"Fine, but if you change your mind, the offer stands."

They reached the apartment and Andie unlocked the door. The repairman was gone, but he'd left some things in the corner, which meant he'd probably be back. Andie took the food from Raesh and placed it inside the fridge. She walked over to the window, back to that great view, and sat on the windowsill. Raesh came over.

"I don't remember inviting you in," she said, smirking.

"Well, I know you needed help bringing in the heavy plate. Plus, I'm not a vampire."

"Oh, can you even imagine living with vampires?"

"Absolutely not, I bet it was terrifying. I'm so glad they got wiped out. I don't know which was worse: the mind controlling or the flying."

"I vote mind control."

"Yeah, but you know what? I'd have fun with that one."

Andie laughed, glad of having made at least one friend. Nothing could ever truly take her mind off her father or the task ahead of her, and she definitely couldn't be distracted from the danger, but Raesh was just the person she needed to meet on the first night. He was kind, friendly, welcoming, and in a way, he reminded her of home. There was something about him that was patient, deliberate. She knew he liked her and he wasn't shy at showing it, but he wasn't pushing himself on her. He was sweet.

"You know, even after the vampires, our parents' generation faced terrible times," he said, his smile fading into a grave expression. "They were all brave. They had to be."

"You mean the terrorist attacks in Taline?"

"And the other thing. The Quelling."

For a moment, Andie stopped breathing.

Not this. Any subject in the world but this. Something in her chest constricted, tightened beyond belief at the thought of what she'd lost and what her father had suffered. Even after eighteen years, it still hurt. There were a lot of things about her family before the Quelling that she had forgotten, but she could never forget the night itself. Never.

"I... I don't even know how to ask this," Raesh began. "I don't even know if I should, but looking at you now, I think I have to. I've heard stories about your father my entire life. Are the rumors true? Was it really a spell that went wrong?"

"I really don't want to talk about that, Raesh," she snapped.

Raesh looked away, embarrassed or ashamed, she didn't know which. She instantly regretted what she'd said and how she'd said it. After all, there was no way he could've understood the emotional pain that she had to endure ever since the accident. Even she could barely understand it, and it was her own pain.

"Look. I'm sorry. I'm just really tired. All the trains I've been on today, I guess. Can we please just continue this conversation later?"

"Ah, the old 'later' ploy, right? How original." He laughed. She laughed, too. Neither of them meant it.

Raesh turned and headed to the door, and Andie watched and wished there was something she could say to make up for the mood she'd ruined. He really had been great to her, and after the dizzying reception she'd gotten when first arriving in the city, she really needed Raesh's comforting presence that night. He turned back at the door.

"We don't need to continue this," he said. "I can see on your face how much it hurts. We can talk about whatever you want. We don't ever need to discuss this again."

He turned to leave and was almost out of the door when she stopped him.

"Raesh. Thank you for sharing with me earlier. About your family and how much you want magic. That was really nice."

He smiled that warm smile of his and left. Andie sighed and leaned back against the wall. She was alone again with her thoughts. Always alone with her thoughts.

ANDIE SAT in bed and prepared to lay down as she watched the reflection of the setting sun bounce off the shining glass walls of the building across the street. She'd gotten everything ready for the next day, and there was nothing left except to be anxious and to implant her icon. She wasn't in a hurry to have the university monitor every move and magical use, but there was no way around it. If she was going to commit to her studies at the University, she had to conform to their rules.

"Here goes my freedom," she said to herself.

She held the icon in the palm of her hand and took a deep, shuddering breath.

"I, Andie Rogers, of sound mind and spirit, do take the oath of the Academy and accept my duties, responsibilities, and limitations as a student of this great body."

As the final syllable passed her lips, the icon rolled over in her hand and vanished under her skin in a soft flash of golden light. At first, she didn't feel anything, even after turning her hand over and making a few fists, but then the cold set in. Then the heat. Together, the impossible sensation of hot and cold flowed through her veins and to her heart, and from there, it was sent through her entire body. She opened her mouth in a silent scream as a violent convulsion made its way from head to toe. The feeling only lasted a moment, though, and it faded with every beat of her heart until she felt perfectly like herself again. She laid back in bed and kicked herself under the covers.

Sleep didn't come easy, but that was unsurprising, and tonight she had even more on her mind. She tried to suppress the memories of what happened to her mother and her father's accident. She tried to trust Mirth, the healer who was staying with her father back home. Of course, there was also her new life in the city to consider. This city that didn't seem as welcoming or as promising as she had hoped. She'd given up trying to see the silver lining in Arvall City after she'd picked up the rest of her books earlier. Thinking of the books made her remember.

She rolled over and reached under the bed to retrieve the bag she'd hidden there earlier. She opened it and then uncovered the secret compartment in the bottom of it. She dropped the bag and opened the book on her lap. It was dusty. *From Dragons to Men*. A history of dragon-blooded people and their magic. She wanted so badly to flip through it with relish, as she did almost every night, but she had enough on her mind. She closed it and locked it away in the cabinet of the nightstand, and slid the key into her pocket.

She laid down again, trying to block out the blackness of her thoughts. But she couldn't suppress them and she knew there was only one way that she would be able to get to sleep. She let it all in, all the worry and pain and memories, and once they rooted themselves deep in her mind, she accepted that everything was her fault. After that, the guilt crushed her into sleep.

She dreamed again. She'd been dreaming the same dream for years and only the way she saw it changed.

It always began the same.

She stared out in front of her, through an odd and exciting haze. Somewhere in the haze, there is a mirror that isn't clear. She can't tell if it was because of the haze or if the mirror itself was somehow... wrong. All she knew was that the mirror was really a window—a sight into some other world or other life—and that she must see through somehow. She has to know what's there to see.

And then a sound. Slight, soft, hardly a sound at all, almost as if it were only made of the most delicate of sounds for certain ears to hear. It was the smallest of echoes.

Over the years, the haze lightened and lifted until finally it subsided. Eventually, she could see a field and a woman standing in the middle of it. Beautiful, majestic, and covered in blood, the woman reached out, maybe to Andie, maybe to the universe, and then fire fell from the sky in terrifying waves of light and flames and brilliant destruction.

The sound cleared as well and revealed itself to be the woman's voice. Louder and louder it grew. She was screaming. The woman in the field who was drenched in blood, who seemed to be destroying the earth, was screaming for help.

Andie woke violently, sweating and breathing as if she'd just finished a race. She was shivering, from fear or sweat it didn't matter. The iridescent pattern on her left arm burned as it always did after the dream. She was thankful that she only had the trace in one spot on her body. For now.

Something compelled her to move, to run, to escape the bed and the room and the apartment. A dark energy that shrouded her mind and made her desperate to clear her head. She jumped out of bed and pulled on her favorite pair of jeans and a faded t-shirt that she had left piled on the floor in her late-night exhaustion, and hurried through her room and into the hallway, slipping on a pair of flats and grabbing a crumpled sweatshirt on her way out. She stopped for a quick breath, a moment to clear her mind and realize that the dream was over. That she was safe.

She didn't know what made her run from her room. It could've been fear, but she was never one to show herself to be a coward. It had to be something more, and maybe she'd never know until she understood the dream itself. She turned and headed down the stairs. Maybe Marvo was up and could make her some coffee at the restaurant. At the bottom of the stairs she halted, shocked by the sight.

The restaurant was completely full; people were everywhere, eating, drinking, or waiting for their order. There weren't even any open chairs. She wondered what they were all doing there so early in the morning, until she looked to the front of the place, where the giant panes of glass that made the storefront showed that it was late morning. The sun was already halfway across the sky. Then she heard laughter. She turned and saw Raesh, posted in the corner with a steaming cup, taking a break or slacking off. He was watching her.

"I was just getting ready to come up and wake you. You're gonna be late."

Andie's eyes widened with the realization that she had slept through the night. Without so much of a glance at her watch, she ran out the door into the warm late-morning light and raced down the cobbled street towards the direction of the University.

Her arm burned and with a mad panic, she realized the iridescent glow on her arm was visible. She desperately pulled on her sweatshirt and tugged down the sleeves to cover the evidence, panting from the exertion of her sudden and unexpected sprint. She couldn't let anyone see.

She contemplated turning back to get her backpack

when she realized she had left it behind, but her legs propelled her ever forward down the long and winding roads of Arvall City, towards the great walls of the University. She ran her hands down her jeans as she walked, and was relieved when she found her class schedule and University map folded in her back pocket. At least she would be able to find her way to class. She held it tightly in her hand as she trudged onward.

She couldn't be late and risk expulsion. Not now. Not when she needed answers the most.

CHAPTER THREE

ANDIE COULDN'T MISS ANOTHER DAY. IF SHE MISSED even one class today, she would blow her shot at learning to control her powers and discover her abilities forever. Nineteen is the oldest age the Academy accepted without a special letter of recommendation, which she had no way of getting, and the first eleven days are the most a student can miss before they forfeit the year. The Academy opens its door on the two hundredth day of each year, and today was the two hundredth and twelfth day. Crunch time.

She raced through the streets toward SKY 6. Without meaning to, her powers manifested in her haste and before she realized it, her magic was pushing people aside and creating a clear path for her. She stopped and checked the icon; it was glowing faintly, warning her against using her magic, but as long as she kept it to small things - and nothing too frequent - she would be okay. Realizing she would never make it in time at this pace, she tried hailing a cab, but not a single one stopped.

All at once, she felt everything: her tardiness, her new life, her anxiety, her hurry, the sights, the sounds, the hard and steady breath of Arvall City, and she felt overwhelmed with the energy and activity.

"So, this is what it's like?" she wondered out loud.

As if in rude answer, someone snatched her folded map from her hand and waved it before her eyes. "What's this, now?" a husky voice taunted her. "An antique, is it? Looks valuable."

Andie glowered at the man. "Not valuable, but I do rather need it. Hand it back."

The man smiled a toothy grin. "Nah, looks of value to me." And with a final wink he turned on his heels and ran back the way Andie had just come.

Her mind was still floating in wonder, but luckily her body reacted on instinct. She turned and was chasing him down the street, across the intersection, around two corners, and finally into an alley. She needed that damn map to get to the University, and she wasn't going to let some petty thief ruin her chances of getting there.

On and on they ran, rounding corners and racing down alleyways. The thief had been tiring steadily, but growing up in a rural area had bred Andie for this moment. She caught him and threw her weight on him. They both came crashing down, but Andie hit her head on the stone of the alley floor. For a moment, she was dazed and the world swam before her eyes while the thief scrambled to his feet and grabbed her map again.

When he saw that Andie had hit her head, he took a moment to catch his breath. He looked down at her and laughed. At least, until he saw the cut on her head begin to heal. He gasped, dropped the map, and took off running as if the great dragon Gordric himself were chasing him. He knew what everyone knew. Healing is a sign of dragon magic. Andie saw the fear on his face and suddenly only that look mattered to her.

"No, wait!" she screamed.

But he was already gone. She cursed herself—her lack of control and her dragon blood—and hoped he would be frightened enough to keep his mouth shut. She stood up and folded the now crumpled map, which was fortunately still in one piece. Why someone would want to steal a piece of paper, she had no idea. She slid it in her back pocket and looked around to regather her bearings.

Now, she had even less time. She turned and started off at a jog, and then she remembered. The icon. She stopped mid-stride and checked her palm. Nothing. It was glowing again, warning her, but no alarm was sounded, no searing pain. It was unbelievable. She couldn't be that lucky. She waited and waited and waited, but nothing happened.

"They must not be able to detect dragon blood," she mused out loud. "That's the only explanation."

After a few more moments of nothing, she started walking again. She decided to simply see how it acted on her way to the Academy. She kept her head low and ran.

Somewhere along her route, after getting lost in the baffling streets of University Park, Andie caught a cab. It dropped her at the train station and she only just managed to board before the doors closed. While she rode the train up the mountain, almost completely vertical, she fixed herself.

All the trains were charmed so that the relative gravity inside the cars didn't change. Everyone could walk around just as they would on level ground. The train seemed to reach the top faster than it had the day before, but she knew it was only her nerves. Once off the train, she was running again, almost leaping to catch the class that started in two minutes. She began to slow as she got closer to the front doors and then she looked up and took a good look at that magnificent black marble.

"You going to come in or just stare at the damn thing?" asked a voice beside her.

Andie turned to face a beautiful girl. She had a

familiar smile. It took Andie a moment to realize that it was familiar because it reminded her of Raesh.

"Are you Carmen?" Andie asked. "Raesh's cousin?"

"Guilty," she said, looking coy as if she knew something she might or might not share. "And you're the prodigy girl with the dad who spelled himself into an almost vegetative state." She shook her head as if watching a kitten try to climb something it couldn't understand was too tall.

Andie's jaw dropped a little at Carmen's complete tactlessness.

"Don't feel bad, sweetie. This is the city. We've all got sad stories here."

"Do you all say what you're thinking without any concern for people's feelings?"

"You're upset. And you have a right to be. Look, I'm sorry, I didn't mean any disrespect to you or your father. I barely have the semblance of a filter. The truth is, that no one in Vall is going to play by your country rules of hospitality and patience. It just won't fly here. But, for my part, I apologize."

"Thanks," Andie said, not quite sure how else to respond to the girl.

Carmen looked Andie over from head to toe, scanning with intense concentration as if she were x-raying her skeleton. Then she looked Andie right in her eyes and smiled that beautiful, warm, familiar smile.

Andie could tell that even if she was uncouth, she was genuine.

"I really should get going," Andie said. "My class is starting practically as we speak."

"Morning classes? Black the stars, girl."

"What?"

"Black the stars. It means something like 'I can't believe it.'"

"Ah. Well, I'll have to catch up on the language, I guess," Andie laughed. "I'll see you around?"

"Yes, you will. I'll be looking out for you. Which is a big deal because it's not something I would normally do, even for a girl my cousin has a crush on." She winked.

"He doesn't have a crush on me," Andie said, suddenly defensive. She looked down at her feet as she felt her face redden, knowing full well that it was true.

"Not sure why you said that or which one of us you think is stupid enough to believe it, but he most certainly does and you know it, don't you?" Carmen asked with a grin. "Just let him down easy."

With that she pushed Andie through the front doors.

CHAPTER FOUR

IT WAS UNREAL. THERE WASN'T A SINGLE DREAM OR mental picture or sprawling fantasy that could capture what Andie saw when she crossed the threshold. She never expected it to be that beautiful. The ceilings, walls, and floors were made of the same black marble as the outside. The doors and fixtures were all made of solid gold. The light—if it could be called that—almost looked like an ethereal glow bleeding from the very marble itself. It was magical. Transformative. It lit the halls and the rooms like no regular light could.

While outside the marble was still the way it should be. Inside, the floors and ceiling seemed to be moving. It was incredible. Once they reached the end of the entrance hallway, the ceiling disappeared into an endless black void. They had passed into the heart of the mountain. Flying over their heads were hundreds, maybe thousands of tiny yellow creatures, zipping back and forth as if they were on a mission.

"Mountain Faeries," Carmen said. "Think of them as little messengers. They handle all correspondence inside the University."

"Fitting, I guess. They never lie, right?"

"Correct. Pretentious little self-righteous snitches if you ask me. That endlessness above us is where you go if you use too much magic outside of school. I'm not sure what happens up there, but I hope I never find out."

They walked on and Andie began to notice just how many students there were. Thousands upon thousands. They were everywhere. Some had skin in hues and tones she'd never seen before, and some she figured were from the north, were so pale they were almost transparent. They were speaking all kinds of different languages, some of which she'd come into contact with before, but most of which she couldn't even begin to decipher.

"How many students are there?" she asked.

"Five, six hundred thousand. Who knows? More just keep coming. That's SKY 1, the faculty train. It runs up to their rent-free homes a little higher up the mountain."

She pointed to a train of silver and gold that was just pulling off from the tiny station in the middle of a vast interior park.

"Down that way is distress training. Farther on is

dangerous species, which is the adjacent wing to extinct species."

"Like dragons," Andie muttered.

"Like dragons," Carmen agreed, squinting at Andie from the corner of her eye. "That way is for students who have graduated from the Academy on to the next levels. That hallway to the far left... well, I don't know what that is, but I'd steer clear. So, how do you feel?"

"It's nothing like what I could've imagined. I've heard stories from my father, even seen pictures, but this is different. Huge. I mean really, really huge. I never made it past the front office yesterday. I feel... kind of insignificant."

"Great. You're already fitting in, then. Although, tomorrow, lose the I'm-a-cute-country-girl aura. You'll never get any worthwhile guys with that act," she said, having another long look at Andie. "Speaking of, if you're thinking about staying around here after dark to make out with a warlock hottie, think again. This place locks down when the moon comes up, and the security is insane."

"Insane?"

"Yeah. I mean animated soldiers of steel and immobilizing mist among others. You ever hear of matrices?"

Of course she had. How could she ever forget those terrible things?

"Yeah. I've heard of them," she said, looking away.

"Well, that's me," Carmen said.

"What is?"

"Oh, you can't hear it? I forgot what it was like to be new here."

Carmen reached over to touch Andie's forehead and traced a small circle. A shot ran through Andie's head and then the sweetest, most alluring song Andie had ever heard rushed through her mind and senses.

"Hear that?" Carmen asked. "That's the siren's call. It'll take you where you need to go. What's yours anyway?"

"I don't know. I didn't even know I had one."

"Yeah. We can listen to each other's, but everyone has their own individual call. I thought it was supposed to be something beautiful, but mine sounds almost like some sort of horn. I guess I got the short stick. See ya, haybale."

Carmen bounded away and Andie was left to fend for herself. She kept listening to the song, but it didn't sound like a horn. It must be her own call. She turned a couple times, trying to find which direction the song was coming from. When she caught it, she just followed it. It was the easiest, most satisfying thing in the world.

The siren's call led her on a winding path into the Academy and around its many corners. It felt right and yet she couldn't understand it; it felt good, even, but she couldn't imagine anything capable of making so sweet a sound. It was like music and laughter and a waterfall all together. It was the single most beautiful sound she'd ever heard. It seemed extravagant to have a specific call for each student, especially when considering that there were six hundred thousand of them.

Andie turned right and found herself walking into a classroom. She was smiling softly, lost in the beauty of the call, and so, for a moment, she didn't notice where she was. After she'd been standing there some moments, she began to look around as her mind focused. It wasn't History of Magic in Noelle. There were potions, bubbling pots, strange and cloying smells, assorted pieces of animals, and hundreds of vials. It was a potions class and she was in the wrong place. She apologized profusely and had to duck several times to avoid the giant, rotating ball of viscous liquid the professor was floating in front of the class.

Back in the hallway, she heard the call again. On and on she went, eventually being led out into a garden on the mountainside. There again, Andie was happily surprised. There were thousands upon thousands of gorgeous, luminous blooms in the garden. Every imaginable flower in every imaginable variety. They were sprouting, hanging, twisting, draping, creeping, and even floating. They were in every color Andie had ever heard of and many more she didn't even know were possible. Some even changed color. Buzzing among the blooms and falling petals were skops. Similar to faeries, but tended flowers and only lived for about twelve days. Andie came upon a row of vibrant green bushes that must have continued at least half a kilometer long. They were brimming with pearlescent flowers that were rising and falling over and over again. As Andie drew closer, she saw that they were actually dying and blooming again in an endless cycle that lasted only a matter of moments.

Shaking herself out of the daze of beauty, Andie began to run. Her class had definitely started by then, and she had no idea if she was even anywhere close to the classroom. There would be plenty of time to explore the Academy later, if she wasn't expelled first.

She ran as hard as she could, weaving through and under the flowers that were everywhere. Her foot caught on something and she fell, slamming chest first into the ground. Her breath fled her. She coughed, having breathed in some dust, and turned.

There was a pair of legs sticking out from under a tangle of roots and peach-colored blooms. The legs bend down onto their knees and they scooted backward out of the roots. A torso then appeared. Then a head. Soon the complete figure was standing over Andie. A perfect, tall figure who smiled down at her with a smile that could melt even the coldest of hearts. He reached out a hand to help her up.

"Were you looking for me?"

CHAPTER FIVE

Andie was so stunned by his looks and his mesmerizing eyes that, at first, she couldn't speak, couldn't even understand that he was trying to help her to her feet. Seeing she wasn't focusing, he bent down and grabbed her by her shoulders. Firmly but gently, he lifted her to her feet and only then did Andie fall back into reality.

She stared dumbly into his eyes, then shook her head and pulled herself from her trance. What was she, some pathetic love-struck teenager? "Gross," she said at the thought.

"I'm sorry?"

She blinked and stared, then felt her face burn a horrible shade or red. "Oh, nothing. Sorry."

"I'm Tarven, a student advisor," he said. "You must be my new recruit. I've been looking for you."

"Um, I don't know. I'm not even sure where I am."

"This is the Academy. You are a sorceress, aren't you?"

"Yes. I mean, I don't know where in the Academy I am. What side of the mountain are we on?"

"West. This is the garden of Victory, the designated garden of the University and the city. I look after it sometimes. I'm really into hortological magic."

"Plant magic," Andie said. "Cool."

"Yeah, I think so. I don't really know how I got into it, though. I was born and raised in Arvall City where everything's stone or glass or iron. Don't get me wrong, I've traveled all over Noelle with my family, but always in urban centers. You'd think I'd want to have little to do with actual nature, but it turned out to be something I was really passionate about."

"I've never met anyone who could do plant magic before," she said, averting her gaze to anywhere but his eyes. "How does it work, exactly?"

"Hortological magic is all about understanding the life of the plant. The breath of its stem, the depth of its bloom, the fragility of its petal. It's about wanting to see the plant grow, not wanting to control it, even though through this kind of magic you *can* control the plant."

"Like the ones I saw coming in, dying and blooming?"

"Exactly. I've studied magic my whole life and

never came across anything as noble and undervalued as plants."

"We share similar sentiments in Michaelson. We still depend on crops out there. Are you the only one with that kind of magic here?"

"Well, there's bound to be at least a couple more in a student body of hundreds of thousands. Speaking of, tell me about yourself. I've heard of Michaelson. It's one of the little farming towns north of here, right?"

"Yeah. Well, I'm nineteen and this is my first day at the Academy. I'm here because I need to learn control."

She had no idea why she told him that.

"I'm highly sensitive to other people's pain," she continued. "I believe people don't care enough about their own history, and I want to be a researcher when I graduate."

"That's great. But I think you're late."

"Oh, no!"

She'd completely forgotten about getting to class. It was so nice talking to him, so nice having a normal conversation with a normal and attractive person who didn't know about her family history. Not that being attractive had anything to do with it. But it was nice speaking to someone, anyone, who didn't know or ask about her father.

Class was probably already half over. She smiled and thanked Tarven, and began jogging off. But she didn't know which way to go anymore. The siren's call had ended. She turned and turned, trying to pick up the trail again.

All of a sudden, she felt a wave of magic rush through her. She checked her icon for a warning, but there was nothing. When she looked up again, the entire garden was on fire.

"Did I do that?" she asked, horrified.

"No," Tarven said. "I did."

"Why?"

"It's kind of my job. This is your first test. If you don't pass it, I'm afraid you'll have to go. Sink or swim here, Andie. Put it out or get out. Consider it a fire drill." A sly grin spread across his face, and she didn't know whether she should laugh or be angry. Confusion was what she ended up settling on.

She was taken aback. She had no idea how to control her magic aside from a handful of small spells and charms. She'd spent her entire life forcing herself to hold back, suppress her natural ability. Now this guy wanted her to master her skills without warning? Impossible. The reason she was there was to learn control, focus, and expansion, and yet, it seemed her journey was over before it began. The fire blazed brighter and hotter by the second. All it would take was one wrong move to accidentally tap into her dragon magic and ruin everything she'd been trying to hide since she was born.

"You have to help me," she said, turning to Tarven

and pleading. "Please. I don't have this kind of control over myself yet. It's the whole reason I'm here."

"I'm sorry, but I'm not allowed. This is your test, Andie. *Yours*. I could feel your power the moment you walked in. It's one of the gifts of studying hortological magic. You can do this. And I'd love if you could stop the fire before it destroys the rose hip. I was going to use that for a pretty amazing spell later on."

She walked away a few paces and closed her eyes, trying to focus. She tried to calm herself, the way her mother used to teach her to do when she was a little girl and would get scared or frustrated. And then it dawned on her. Dragons are drawn to fire. It calms them, makes them feel safe, can even heal them in certain situations. She had dragon blood running in her veins. She stretched her hands out to her sides and then it began to fill her. The peace of the flames. She began to feel more powerful, more brave as the flames grew around her. It was almost as if the flames were calling to her. She needed a balance. She needed to embrace the flames and their power without succumbing to the dragon magic.

For the first time, she noticed the other people in the garden. Not many, but enough to make a small crowd. They were pushing together into a little group, trying to avoid the flames and also trying to watch Andie to see what she would do. She wondered if they were forbidden from helping, too.

They were staring at her wide-eyed, no doubt

wondering why she felt so at ease so close to flames. She didn't even feel the heat. But she couldn't reveal that to Tarven. She tried to focus, knowing that if she failed this first task, not only would she be kicked out of the Academy, she would also hurt her father.

What was worse, if she pushed her own magic back down far enough so that the flames burned her as proof that she wasn't immune, she would hurt herself in front of Tarven and who knows what her body would do to naturally heal itself. That was not something he or anyone here could see. The panic began to rise again, but she listened to the flames and remained calm. She took a moment to close her eyes and think.

"Water," she whispered. "Water is in the plants."

She reached out toward the plants on either side of her and flexed her fingers. She focused on the sorcerer's magic inside of her, and did everything in her power to push away her dragon blood instinct. Every stem and bloom stood straight up. She made fists of her hands and all the plants leaned over toward her, releasing every ounce of moisture they had and turned brown, then black in the process. When all the water had been collected in floating pools above her, she used her powers to magnify it and then made it rain inside the garden. Within moments, the fire had been extinguished.

"Very impressive," Tarven said, smiling at her. "And look, you saved the rose hip."

For a moment, Andie couldn't focus. She was

reeling a bit from the loss of the flames. All their comfort, promise, and power had fled with them. Her hands stayed in the air beside her for a moment.

"Andie. Andie, are you okay?" Tarven asked, laying a hand on her shoulder.

She snapped back into the moment, the garden, the circumstance.

She stood still, silent for a long while, and then reeled. "What kind of twisted games are you playing here?" she shouted, rounding on Tarven and locking eyes with him. "You could have burned me to death. I could've died! I'm a first-year Academy student who hasn't even taken one class. I don't even have control of my magic, yet. What if I'd lost control? Do you have any idea what could have happened?" She thought of all the weird, pathetic excuses that a first-year student could possibly use, and spewed them out at him as angrily as she could manage. She hoped it was enough to cover up any evidence of her dragon blood magic that might have seeped out during the exercise.

Andie's heart pounded in her chest as her mind raced with the thought of what would have happened had she actually lost control and hurt herself. Her dragon magic would have healed her, of course, and had she been at home or somewhere isolated, it wouldn't have been a problem. But in front of another person, especially in the University, that was the most dangerous thing she could possibly think of happening.

She swallowed and cleared her throat, all the while glaring at Tarven in front of her.

She hoped he had bought her distress as being caused by fear of being hurt, rather than what she was truly hiding.

Tarven held up his hands to calm her, but he took a few steps back. He claimed to be able to sense her power. He surely must've known to treat her carefully in that moment.

"Okay, easy now. I'm not allowed to interfere as long as the situation is controllable and it looks like you still have a chance to complete the task. Rest assured, no one was going to burn alive today and I would've been right here if something had gone wrong with your magic. Also, your icon measures your distress levels and if it had gotten too high, the entire school board would have teleported in. There was never any real danger, Andie. I promise."

Andie rubbed her eyes with the palms of her hands as she inhaled a deep breath and exhaled slowly. She hadn't even been to her first class yet, and she had nearly revealed herself. What was she doing here? She was in way over her head. "You just pushed it too far, okay?"

"It wasn't like—"

"Just… Don't do anything like that to me again. Please. I wasn't ready."

"I'm sorry, Andie. It was just a test. From the

moment you walked in, I knew you would have been able to handle it just fine."

Andie felt stupid and angry, not so much with him as with herself. She would need to prepare herself for surprises like this. She couldn't afford to slip up. Her life depended on this. "Well, you were wrong."

She cursed herself for sounding like such a snarky brat, but better that he thinks of her as a whiney first-year than as someone with dragon blood. The first, she could deal with, although the situation wasn't exactly ideal. The second, would end up getting her killed.

Tarven was silent then. He kept opening his mouth to respond, but something told Andie that he hadn't even fully considered the circumstances, which was even worse because he went along with the plan without thinking for himself. Andie shook her head.

"Well, I'll say one thing for my first day at the Academy," she said. "At least, it hasn't been dull." She managed a half laugh at that, and Tarven nearly smiled in return. His smile quickly turned to a frown when her expression turned back to one of utter seriousness.

"Well, goodbye then." With that, she turned to leave, mumbling a few awkward parting words about going to the library to prepare for her next class.

CHAPTER SIX

Andie took the long way around, relishing in the cool fresh air that calmed her as she walked. She shook her head at how stupid and ill prepared she had been. Next time, she would be more confident. She would need to learn how to handle surprises and stressful situations without the risk of drawing on her dragon blood magic. She didn't have a choice. When she reached the end of the path, she turned and headed back towards the building.

She'd barely made it back inside when she realized she had no idea where to find her class. This place was massive and going on an exploratory walk would waste time she didn't have. She squeezed her eyes shut in concentration and rubbed her temples with her fingers, doing her best to think of a plan. She couldn't be late. Her eyes flashed open when an idea struck her. She held up her palm and used the opposite hand to press down on the light where the icon was. She closed her eyes and thought of the library. Sure enough, within seconds she could hear the siren's call. She opened her eyes and began to walk.

It took a while to find it, what with dodging the Mountain Faeries, weaving through the seemingly endless crowds, and listening in on other student's siren's call out of curiosity. When she finally found it, there was no mistaking it. The doors had to be at least fifty feet tall, made of what looked like Bleak Oak— wood as black as the night sky—inlaid with gold. The gold had been laid in fractal patterns of exploding curves, and, as Andie neared the doors, she could see the patterns were moving. She couldn't help smiling as she pushed open the door, which, even with its great size, was as easy to open as a regular-sized door.

She couldn't believe it. She was finally there. Leabherlann. The largest and best of the world's repositories. There was no library, no archive, no collection anywhere on the face of the earth that could rival that one. Leabherlann wasn't even half as old as most of the other libraries, yet, it was the greatest. Unparalleled. Andie had been desperate to get there. Inside were rows upon rows of gold and granite desks lined up straight down the center of the room and going back so far that Andie couldn't see the end. Above them were many, many more floors, all with the same incredibly long rows. At first, she thought the other floors were floating, but then she remembered that those were the famous invisible floors of the library.

To the right and left of the desks were the collections themselves. Stone cases that were so tall it was believed they rose hundreds of feet up into the mountain. It had been said that there was no subject, no personage, no branch of magic or its study that could not be found within those great walls. If it wasn't there, it probably didn't exist. Andie took several minutes to absorb the majesty of the place and then she headed for the main desk, a grandiose gold and silver dais whose powerful and beautiful turning gears were as much for function as embellishment. The entire thing was placed in a sunken area in the center of the space.

"Hi," she said, to which she received no answer. "I'm here to do some research."

The woman behind the desk looked at Andie as if what she'd said was the dumbest phrase ever uttered. Andie realized that hundreds of thousands of students came here to do research every single day.

"Oh, sorry," she said. "I want to know where to find the collections. I'd like to read on the dra-"

She stopped herself, knowing it was better to keep her subject to herself.

"I'd like to read on extinct bloodlines."

"Show me your icon access," the woman said, monotone and uninterested.

"My what?"

"I-con ac-cess," she said as condescendingly as possible.

"She's new, doesn't have it yet. I have clearance to let her use mine for the time being."

Andie turned to the sound of the voice and saw Carmen grinning. She walked up to the desk and turned her palm toward the woman, who, reluctantly, swiped her own palm in front of Carmen's.

"Go on," the woman said, returning her attention to whatever was below the silver barrier that Andie couldn't see. Carmen took her by the arm and led her off.

"Good old Murakami," she said. "Never smiled or said a nice thing a day in her life. But she's pureblooded Raeynese."

"You're kidding. The Raeynese Empire was destroyed soon after Hightowyr. I didn't think there were any left."

"Very few, and they've been reduced to intermarriage, with terrifying results."

"Don't you have class right now?" Andie asked.

"Don't you?"

Carmen led her to the elevator and it carried them up to the hundred and first floor. They got out and Andie had to catch her breath. She had thought they were falling, but it was just the invisible floor. She looked down between her feet at the many levels and students beneath her.

"Cool," she said.

Carmen took her back a few cases and pointed her to a particular case.

"This is it?" Andie asked, a bit disillusioned.

"Sure. If by 'this' you mean the entire floor. You can start wherever you want."

And just like that she turned to leave.

"Carmen, wait. Thank you for helping me get in and for bringing me up here. How did you get me in, anyway?"

"I do some work as amanuensis for my bloodlines professor. He's always having me pull a book on some long dead ethnicity or culture. Gives me special access."

"Nice."

She was about to leave again when she turned back. She watched Andie for a moment.

"Be careful who sees you reading up here, Andie. An interest in bloodlines isn't really something people will understand. Even my professor is sort of a pariah. Don't talk about this with anyone."

And she left.

Andie was a bit shaken by Carmen's warning, but she went on anyway. She searched and searched, but even after half an hour she hadn't been able to find a single book on dragons, dragon blood, or the dragonborn. She went back and forth, from case to case to case, and even triple checked the floor's catalogue. There wasn't a single book on anything having to do with dragons. It was like the University was purposely keeping secrets, which was probably the truth. Eventually, tired of searching and thoroughly disappointed, she resigned herself to reading something for class.

Not too long after that, Carmen came back. She brought a friend with her. Yara. Yara was a rather plain girl, but her personality was as magnetic as Carmen's and she was as bookish as Andie wanted to be. Carmen kept looking at Andie when she thought no one was watching, and Andie got the impression that Carmen had come back because she was genuinely worried. Yara kept them both engaged with her stories and endless knowledge of all sorts of things.

"Yara, how do you know so much about Goulstnach?" Andie asked.

"Are you kidding? Those things freak me out. The sadder they get, the bigger they get and it's notoriously difficult to comfort them. Once they reached their limit, they explode and send poisonous pieces of their spine in every direction. Are you telling me that doesn't freak you out?"

"Well, they do now. I'm never going up the mountain."

"Good girl. Also, I couldn't help but notice the book you're reading. I'm pretty sure there's an older version of that that has a professor's note in it. Could be helpful." Yara winked.

"Thanks, Yara."

Just then, Andie heard her siren's call. It was time for her next class.

"I hear my call. It was great talking with you. I hope I can catch up with you again soon."

"You, too," Yara said. "And good luck with the rest of your day."

"Thanks. Thank you, too, Carmen."

"My pleasure. See you later, haybale."

Andie got in the elevator and took it back down to the ground floor. When she stepped out, she couldn't tell which direction the call was coming from. She'd heard there were at least a hundred different entrances to Leabherlann, and so she figured the call must be leading her to another one. But the farther she walked, the more unsure she became. Sometimes she thought she was following the voice, other times it seemed to be coming from behind or to the side of her. Eventually, she found herself down another floor in the archives. The air was thick with dust, the lighting ample but odd, and there didn't seem to be anyone else around. She started reading every plaque, searching for any way out.

Soon, she came across things like *Most Educated and Illustrious Serpents* and *Poisons that Attack only the Soul* and even *Great Magical Shifts of the Third and Fourth Cycle*s. She had inadvertently come upon the special and rare collections, and she was fascinated. There were all kinds of unimaginable subjects. Things she'd heard of only in legend. All that made her wonder if she should even be down there.

At the end of an inordinately long path, a bridge of sorts, she came upon another door, Bleak Oak with a gold inlay just like the much larger one upstairs. She was standing in front of it, debating whether or not to knock when she heard voices. She dropped everything in her hands. It was the same voices that had been haunting her dreams.

"What are you doing?"

The sound of a voice behind her nearly made Andie jump through the ceiling. It took her a moment to get her heart out of her throat. She turned around to see Tarven. With her head full of the siren's call and the voices, she hadn't heard him approach.

"Are you seriously dead-set on freaking me out every time you see me?" she snapped. "Honestly, I'm starting to think your sole purpose here is to make me lose my cool. And why do I keep seeing the same people everywhere?"

"Heh, sorry. Calm down. I wasn't up to anything nefarious. I just saw you over here. Students aren't allowed to be here."

Andie took a moment to breathe and to return her heart rate to normal. She stared at him, wide-eyed.

"I figured that. I just got lost."

"Well, follow me. I'll get you back." He smiled at her and picked up a book that had fallen nearest to him.

Andie bent down to pick up her books and snatched the book out of Tarven's hands as she eyed him suspiciously. "I'll take that, thanks."

Tarven shrugged and led her back the way she'd come and then locked the door behind them.

CHAPTER SEVEN

THE REST OF THE DAY PASSED WITHOUT INCIDENT. Andie enjoyed the rest of her classes—or, at least, as much as she could, considering she was convinced that the same voices from her nightmares were circulating the underground archives at the University—and met some really interesting fellow students.

She made it home that afternoon and settled in for a couple hours of studying, during which time she mostly worried and didn't study. After two hours, the only information she'd managed to absorb was the first sentence of the first paragraph of one of her critical texts. She'd have to finish later, though. She'd promised to have dinner with Raesh and Carmen downstairs.

When she went down, she was a bit early, which gave her some time to talk with Marvo about his family and hers. He told her some stories about her parents and the times they'd had so many years before. He remembered her mom as beautiful, kind, and one of the most generous people he'd ever met. As much as it hurt, she always loved hearing stories about her mother.

Somewhere along sharing his memories, Andie stopped him. Thinking about everything she'd lost wouldn't do. Especially, not every single day. She'd come to the city and to school with the intention of making sure the past didn't repeat itself and building a new kind of life for herself and her father. She had to learn to let go at some point. Besides, Raesh and Carmen would be there soon and she didn't want to be depressed when they showed up. Marvo kissed her cheek and left, looking a bit embarrassed, but understanding.

Carmen came first. She'd been just a couple of neighborhoods over, hanging out with some friends. She had no idea where Raesh was.

"So, what's the deal? You gonna wire my cousin or what?"

"I don't know what that means, but I think the answer's going to be no."

"Wire. It means hook up with."

"What? No. I barely even know him. I'm not gonna sleep with him."

"Whoa, whoa, easy, haybale. I meant date, not sleep with. Thanks for that image, though. Bleh."

"Anyway, what about you? Who do you... wire with?"

"My professor."

Andie paused, completely taken aback.

"Your professor? Are you serious?"

"Possibly."

Carmen grinned. Andie couldn't help herself and she smiled, too.

"Tell you what," Carmen said. "Be nice to me and I'll show you how to turn off your icon."

Andie paused. "Wait, what? We can do that?"

"Well, obviously, we're not supposed to, and we can get into serious trouble if they find out, but how are they supposed to manage each and every one of their hundreds of thousands of icons? Not to mention, thousands of students graduate or transfer all the time and thousands more come in. The trick is not to turn it off completely. We'll just kind of dampen it."

"That is so cool."

The bell over the door rang and in walked Raesh, as handsome and magnetic and awkward as ever. He waved to his dad and came to sit with them.

"What's up, my two favorite ladies?"

"There's a secret door in the underground archives that's holding voices from my nightmares."

Raesh's mouth hung slightly open to complete the look of utter bewilderment on his face. And for the first time since Andie had met her, Carmen was at a complete and total loss for words. Both she and her cousin simply stared at Andie dumbfounded.

"I'm sorry. I guess I could've said hi first. It's just that I've been holding it in all day and didn't have anyone to tell, so I figured I could tell you two here at dinner. Then, I was waiting on you to show up, Raesh, and when you came in my wall just kind of crumbled and I spat it out. I'm really sorry. It's just that even though you're both so different from me, you both seem like you can be trusted."

Carmen's look changed some, becoming more of a look of warmth, but with deeper concern than confusion. But she still couldn't speak.

"Okay," Raesh finally said. "How can we help?"

"Really?"

"You said we look trustworthy, right? Trust us," Carmen said.

"Thank you," Andie said. She tried to formulate her thoughts enough to explain what was going on to them without sounding like a complete crazy person. "Okay, so. I've been having these dreams. Dreams unlike anything I've ever felt before. I used to call them weird, but they're more than that. They're like something from another life. Totally terrifying. And I mean real, paralyzing fear. In the dreams, there are these voices. These otherworldly voices. I don't know what they're saying or what they want, but when I was down in the archives today, I heard those same voices making the same whispers. They were behind some door down there. I didn't see who was making the voices or anything, but I know what I heard."

Andie took a breath and let it out slowly as the weight of what she had been hiding lifted from her shoulders. She then added, "don't bother mentioning that the archives are a restricted area. I know that already."

Raesh and Carmen shared a look and then watched Andie. She waited for one of them to speak.

"So, what do you think?" she pressed when no one spoke.

"Honestly? I don't want to make light of your problems, but I think maybe you're reaching," Carmen said. "And just hear me out. I think you've got a lot going on back home and in your past, and you also just moved to Arvall—which we all know is not kind on the nerves—and started your first year at the Academy. Not to mention, the school board's little entrance exam. I don't deny that you might've heard something down there, but I don't think it was voices from your dreams. I think you've been expecting too much of yourself."

Andie sighed. Of course, they didn't believe her.

"Andie, I'm more worried about you getting in trouble," Raesh said. "First, you missed almost two weeks of school, then you're looking up books you shouldn't be, then you're walking around a restricted area. I think you're pushing your luck. And I agree with Carmen. I think you're just under tremendous strain."

"So, neither of you believe me?"

"It's not that we think you're crazy or anything, it's just that you're asking us to believe something pretty big," Carmen said.

"If you hear it again, or if you find something, let us know," Raesh said. "And above all, watch yourself."

At that exact moment, Marvo happened to be walking by. When he heard Raesh cautioning Andie, he stopped dead.

"What does he mean 'watch yourself?'" Marvo asked.

Even though she barely knew him, Andie suddenly felt like she'd disappointed him. He was beginning to feel like the extension of her dad in Arvall City. She couldn't even meet his eyes.

"Andie, if you're into something you shouldn't be, you need to step away. I'm not your dad, and I'm not trying to be, but you're beautiful and bright and you've already had so much happen in your life. You're here to go to the Academy, learn, and go back home to be with your father. Anything outside of that is a distraction. I don't want to meddle in your life, and I know you're an intelligent and capable young woman, but I'm asking you now, to stay within the lines. Your father made me promise to watch over you. I know you don't want to upset your father."

"You're right," she said, feeling even worse. "I'll be sure to watch myself."

Marvo didn't move. He just kept watching Andie, probably waiting to see if something would show in her face to indicate that she was being less than truthful. Yet, when Andie finally met his gaze, he seemed convinced. He smiled the same warm smile his son had inherited and walked away.

Inside herself, Andie wondered if she was truly going to watch herself or if she had been lying to everyone, including herself.

Or maybe she truly was just crazy and overwhelmed, and she had imagined the whole thing. Somehow, she doubted that.

As NIGHT CREPT NEARER, Andie decided to lay down early. She'd been trying to study practically all day, but her mind simply wouldn't focus. She couldn't stop thinking of those voices ringing through the dark of the archives. Talking to Raesh and Carmen had assuaged her some, but she couldn't tell if it was the two of them that helped her or the fact that she talked to other human beings. On the other hand, the conversation had actually made things somewhat worse. They'd rattled her so much that now she was unsure of what she'd heard. It was an institution of magic, after all, and it was centuries old. Those voices—were they even *voices*, or just noises in the walls? —could have been anything. They might even have been real people. She'd never opened the door. What gave her the right to draw conjectures?

Of course, none of that worry went away just because she wanted to sleep. For a long time, she lay there, anxious, confused, and yet still incredibly hopeful. She really wanted to start over, to let go. She was still holding onto hope that she would find some books in the University that would tell her something about her past and her blood. She wanted to know more about herself, her powers, and who she was supposed to be. Maybe then, she could decipher her dreams. And whether those had been voices or not in the archives, she wanted to know more about them, too.

She unlocked the cabinet next to the bed to retrieve *Dragons*. She flipped through the book, skimming the mix of legend and fact, tracing the incredible sketches of dragons with her fingers and feeling a void in her life where the totality of the history of her bloodline should've been. There was something in the back of the book, too. A sort of makeshift family album that her dad had put together for her just before she left. She flipped through those pages, too, stopping once and again to read some of the words her mother had written on a picture or in a letter. She looked through the pictures, seeing herself as she truly was in all her dragon blood glory; colored hair and eyes and all. It was the dragon side she'd been forced to keep locked away inside. She almost didn't recognize herself anymore.

Sometime later, she finally fell into an uneasy sleep.

CHAPTER EIGHT

TIME PASSED. HOURS BECAME DAYS AND DAYS BECAME weeks. Andie settled into a rhythm and things began to go well. There was school, Raesh, Carmen, Marvo, breakfast and dinner at the restaurant, and a lot of good days. The time passed quietly. Andie finally got to a place where she could focus on her studies and do good work. She never missed class, never turned in an assignment late, and had gotten excellent marks in every class. She was slowly meeting more and more new people, and even knew quite a few well enough to call them friends, but Raesh and Carmen were her best friends. They were simply right for her.

Things with her dad at home were pretty good, too. He hadn't gotten any worse and had even improved some, and they'd been in contact much more. The only part of her life that still wasn't right was the voices she'd heard. For the most part, she'd been able to move on from the things she couldn't change, but there was something about those voices that just wouldn't let go of her no matter what she did. She'd gone back to Leabherlann many times, and even tried to get back into the archive. She never found anything, though.

She'd nearly given up, then something happened in her History of Modern Magic class.

"Good morning, ingrates," the professor sneered. "I want you all to know how thrilled I am to be here with you, again, for another wonderful day of unrewarding and futile attempts to give your minds shape and your lives purpose. Look at you, already burnt-out and you aren't even old enough to have been really chewed up and digested by the filthy, malicious, maggot-ridden world that wants you dead or dying. Cheers."

The professor for that class was cynical, to say the least. He also often smelled of booze. He was a self-proclaimed nihilist and he clearly hated his job. It was anyone's guess why he continued to come to work. He was so uninterested in his students that he had never even allowed them to know his name. He cared nothing for order or work in general. He alternated between long periods of no classroom work or homework at all to consecutive days of grueling, soul-crushing work. He was undeniably brilliant, but arguably the most unpleasant, offensive, pessimistic, and angry person in

Arvall City. Of all Noelle, even. Maybe even of Shaeyara, itself.

"So, I'm sure you've been wondering about this giant blank space in your syllabi. That is, if you haven't been rendered completely worthless by your inability to comprehend the nature of this course and your age group's general bewilderment. We've now come to the point in our class, excuse me, *my* class where it's time to learn about dragons, dragonborn, dragon blood, dragon magic... so on. All things dragon. Yay."

Andie couldn't believe it. She sat bolt upright in her chair and almost screamed from sheer excitement. She'd spent weeks scraping everywhere for even a hint of dragons and now it looked as if everything she ever wanted to know was about to be delivered to her without the least effort.

"Oh, by the way, the school board and the city council and the major governor and the chancellor and every other person whose designation makes them feel important doesn't want you to learn this. Screw them."

Andie was ecstatic. This was one of the reasons she'd most wanted to come to school. She didn't think she could sit still, she was so excited. She readied her pen and notepad.

"Let's start with a basic summary even you degenerates can't fail to grasp. Dragons were gigantic, ferocious, man-eating beasts who plagued the world for thousands upon thousands of years. During their time, there was no such thing as peace. No such thing as safe. They took countless lives for no reason at all. They were a curse and demonic presence on the earth, and the best thing they ever did for us was die off from inbreeding."

Andie's excitement faded. She'd been so overzealous that she'd actually written down everything up to "safe." She couldn't understand what he meant. She thought he had to be playing a sick joke or twisting the truth.

"The worst thing they ever did was manage to get their blood into human bodies, creating the most obscene and dangerous abominations in history. I'm talking about an entire race of people who were angry and evil. As a matter of fact, they weren't even people. You societal rejects aren't too much better, but who am I to judge..."

This wasn't right. She just kept thinking to herself that this wasn't right.

She knew her people, her heritage, had been persecuted and hunted throughout history. She knew that her having dragon blood magic was enough to get her killed. But she had been sure, so sure deep in her heart, that there must have been some great mistake in history. How could an entire race be evil? She didn't feel evil. She knew her mother wasn't evil. She was sure there was more to it than what the world has been led to believe. There must be.

"Luckily for you human stains, the world was

purged. The dragons and their foul human spawn were all eradicated. The dragons were killed by some mysterious method that has been lost to history, but we know how the dragonborn died. Hanging. Drowning. Evisceration. Decapitation. Several unsightly and shockingly grotesque spells. The culling wasn't gentle, and we know for a fact..."

Andie didn't want to believe it, any of it. The professor went on and on about the dragons and the dragonborn and all the atrocities they committed. For a while, Andie was totally set against his philippic, but the more she listened, the more she began to wonder. What did she really know about the dragons and their keepers? All she knew was the very little contained in *Dragons* and the stories that her dad had told her. But he'd admitted time and time again over the years that he'd never known anyone with dragon blood other than her mother, who knew next to nothing about their long heritage.

Was it possible they had been completely unaware of the truth? After all, the entire world had banded together to annihilate the dragons and all of the dragonborn people.

There had been no international effort like that in all of recorded history. There must have been a truly great evil about for every living soul on the planet to want them gone. Andie thought long and hard about what she knew of dragons, which was essentially nothing except that they were massive, powerful, and extremely dangerous. Then the worst possible thought came into her mind. Could her parents have outright lied? Maybe the dragons and the dragonborn truly were evil.

After class, feeling completely heartsick and nauseous all at the same time, Andie returned to the University's vast collection of books to make one final, fleeting attempt to find some more information. Even though she remembered how the professor had said everyone was against this subject being taught, she held hope that there was at least one volume somewhere in there. Of course, without Carmen there to provide access, she couldn't even take the elevator to the bloodlines floor. Fortunately, she ran into Yara.

"Hey, Andie. Wow, you look like total crap."

"Oh, yeah. Thanks," Andie half smiled and rubbed her neck awkwardly. "It's just that I've really been trying to find something in here and I'm not having any luck. I'm just going to give up."

"Maybe I can help," Yara said, smiling ear to ear. "What are you looking for?"

"Honestly? Something on dragons or the dragonborn."

Yara caught her breath and inadvertently took a step back. For a moment, she just stared.

"Carmen told me you might be interested in something like that," she said. "Please just tell me it's for an assignment or something."

Andie nodded quickly. "Of course, what else would it be for?"

Yara eyed her suspiciously but then nodded. "Okay. Look, I don't know much, but I do know they keep some books in the back. Some stuff they really don't want any students to see. Down deep in archives, hidden. You might find some interesting things there. There are old, damaged books there, but they also hide things there. Every now and again, a student sneaks down to find a 'dirty' book. I'm not sure what they mean by dirty. Anyway, I just saw a professor come out. Maybe the door is still open. Try giving it a good push."

"Thank you, Yara. I'm kind of going out of my mind here."

"Don't mention it."

Yara walked away slowly, as if afraid of something she'd done, while Andie hurried off to find the entrance to the archives. She walked so quickly she almost ran. She didn't even slow down when the heads began to turn, but she did remember that she was wearing the icon and she wasn't sure what kind of surveillance the thing provided. The last thing she needed was the school board sending someone to check on her. Yet, she couldn't stop herself from moving toward the archives.

She finally reached the door and, just as Yara had said, it gave when Andie pushed it. She looked around the space to make sure no one was there and just managed to see two professors talking in excited whispers behind the first bookcase. She crouched low behind an abandoned desk and waited for them to leave. She realized how heavily she was sweating and how quickly her heart was racing.

"Calm down, Andie," she whispered to herself. She took a deep breath to calm herself and calm her breathing. The last thing she needed was to be found there. Or, even worse, to be questioned about why she was so agitated.

Within a few moments, the professors were on their way out and Andie was alone. She crept into the room and closed the door behind her. The archives, though intimidating and poorly lit, were as breathtaking as they had been on her first visit. Even in her heightened excitement, she had to take a moment to appreciate the place.

Now that she wasn't being distracted by trying to follow the siren's call, she could focus more precisely on what was in the room. The main path through the archives was a raised wooden bridge of sorts, with stairs leading up or down to the sections the path ran beside. She'd almost completely ignored the collections to the left of the bridge the last time she was there. There were haphazard piles of books that must have been at least forty feet tall, and careless stacks of paper thrown about on the tables and the floor, as if someone kept meaning to organize, but seemed to forget each time a new stack came in. It didn't look to Andie like anyone had organized those archives in decades. Without even knowing where to begin, Andie walked about halfway across the massive bridge, took a set of stairs to the lower floor, and began rummaging through the shelves.

She must've been there over an hour, searching and taking down, and guessing. She'd had no luck, not even a hint of what she'd wanted to know. She couldn't help wondering if she'd have had better luck by calling Carmen. She needed someone else down there to help her look, but if some professor walked through, she didn't want Carmen getting in trouble over something so stupid.

It was quite a while before she found something that she thought might prove worthwhile. A large, dusty tome with an embossed dragon on the cover. Her heart nearly skipped a beat as she ran her fingers over the textured cover. Behind it were three more books with similar markings on the front. She couldn't help but laugh out loud to herself, easing the tension she had felt build in the pit of her stomach since she arrived in the archives. But just as she was flipping through the opening pages and getting excited, the bells rang to signal that the University would soon be closing for the night.

She looked about to make sure no one could see her, and then she hid the dusty old books in her backpack and headed for the door.

CHAPTER NINE

SHE GOT HOME LATER THAN USUAL THAT NIGHT, BUT SHE was ecstatic to have finally found books on dragons. She came in and threw off her things in a tornado of eagerness and self-congratulation. Just as she was settling in her chair with dinner and preparing to eat while she read, her phone buzzed.

"It's me," he said. "You busy?"

Andie stared at the screen at the unfamiliar number. "Who?"

"Tarven. Who else?"

Andie rolled her eyes. "Seriously, you're calling me at home? How did you even get my number?"

He ignored her questions.

"Are you ever going to forgive me for the fire? It's been weeks now. I only did what they told me to do. I don't know what to say to you, Andie. I was there, I would've helped if necessary. I promise."

Andie thought for a moment. He was right. It had been weeks and she knew he'd only done what he'd been told to do. She'd been threatened with expulsion if she failed. She was sure he had been threatened with something similar. That still didn't explain why he was calling her now.

"So, you busy?" he asked.

"Well, I sort of... actually... it depends. What do you need?"

"Nothing, really. Just need to see a pretty face and have fun with a super smart girl. You up for drinks?"

Andie rolled her eyes. "I don't really know about that. I'm busy with homework, and have so much to catch up on."

"Swamped with school work already? The year has barely started." Tarven's laugh was magnetic, but she forced herself not to smile. She wasn't going to be swooned that easily, especially by a guy who almost caused her to out herself.

"Not really, just... Oh, why not. I could use the distraction. It'll be low key, right?" She knew she had to stay in and study. Her mind was dead-set on pouring through her new books. Her words betrayed her.

"As low key as anything I do."

"Fair enough. When and where?"

"Plaza One. Quarter to midnight."

"Whoa, that's kind of-"

Tarven had already hung up.

"-late," she finished.

She knew she shouldn't, that she had so much more important work to do, but, for some reason, hearing his voice made her feel like she had to go. She slipped into some different clothes, grabbed her purse, checked to make sure the icon was still turned off, and headed out the door.

She met Tarven and his friends at the Plaza One bar and they all started chatting. As with what usually happens in large groups, they eventually broke down into smaller groups, or even pairs, with separate conversations. Andie drank, but sparingly, whereas Tarven drank without restraint and without showing anything more than the most benevolent symptoms of his intoxication.

"So, where exactly are you from, Andie Rogers?" Tarven asked.

"Michaelson," she said. "But you knew that already."

Tarven grinned at her. "Where in Michaelson, I mean."

"Oh. At the southern shore of Gordric's Pain."

"Ah, so you're of the Gordric's Pain Rogers? That's good stock, I hear."

Andie laughed and rolled her eyes at him as she took another moderate sip of whipper's beer, a special brew only sold in Arvall City. All Andie, or anybody else for that matter, knew about the beer was that its process was quick, and its recipe called for, among other things, watermelon rinds and extract of orchid. It took her a while to get used to the sweet taste. Marvo would serve it at the restaurant on weekends, and it had quickly grown to be one of her favorite drinks.

"So, who is Andie Rogers, other than a girl who hates fire?"

"I'm a first-year student at the Academy and I like history." She smirked as it was his turn to roll his eyes. Andie couldn't help but smile as she mentally admitted to herself that she did deserve some time to unwind. Plus, a little flirting never hurt anyone. It had been ages since she even had time to think about anything other than her father, and she set her mind to doing everything she could to enjoy her night.

"Interesting. Historical events or timeless wars?"

"Hmm... wars."

Tarven raised his eyebrow. "Interesting. Now we're getting somewhere. What makes a girl so worried about her peers' safety so interested in war?"

"Nothing so grand as what you're imagining, I'm sure. I just find the destruction and beauty of war fascinating."

"Beauty?"

"Yes. Nothing unites people like a war. The bigger, the longer, the worse the war, the closer the survivors will be. War brings love and hope and significance to the surface. And sure, it's bloody, cruel, and most of the time it's fought over nothing, but, when it's over, the world needs to heal itself and sometimes, given the right circumstances, that can be—"

"Beautiful," Tarven finished, watching her like he'd never seen her before. "Okay, I think I'm beginning to understand you. But, just to play devil's advocate, the aftermath of war isn't always so welcoming."

"I know that better than most," she said.

Tarven watched her. She hadn't meant to say it out loud. After that, she put her drink down. Letting hints of her personal vicissitudes slip out was evidence she'd had enough.

"I just think war is one of those things that defines an age. Every age. You know?"

"I get you," he said. "Speaking of age, you're nineteen, right? The Academy starts accepting students at the age of sixteen. Why'd you wait so late?"

"Obligations," she said, somewhat more ominously than she'd meant.

"Can I ask what kind?"

Andie was silent. She wasn't trying to ignore him, she just honestly didn't know how to respond. Other than the one slip, she'd been exceptionally careful not to reveal anything personal all night. Still, Tarven was beginning to seem like he could be trusted. After all, he hadn't told anyone he found her in the archives.

"I don't mean to pry, and you don't have to answer if you're not comfortable, but did your obligations have to do with your father?"

She turned to look at him, right in his eyes. There was no malice there.

"How do you know about my father?"

"This is the University, Andie. People talk. Rumors spread. There's hardly anything about anybody that most of the students and faculty don't know."

He eyed her as he spoke and she felt her heart rate pick up slightly. Was he suggesting that he knew more about her than he initially led on? She narrowed her eyes at him and clenched her teeth.

"He had an accident," she said, bringing the conversation back around to her father. She wouldn't give him the opportunity to ask more questions about her. Not if it meant the risk of her outing herself. "He overwhelmed himself with too much magic. He hasn't been the same since. Honestly, I don't know how it happened. My mother died when I was young and my father hasn't really been the same ever since."

She stopped there. She cursed herself. Tarven did seem trustworthy, but she still hadn't really made up her mind whether or not she should share with him, and, even then, what pieces of the truth he could be trusted with.

"How did your mom die?"

He asked it gently, sympathetically, but she couldn't help thinking that she may have said too much already.

"She... I... we never really... it was... someone came... and... she was on the ground... I saw her... I... we..."

She was scrambling and even her breathing was beginning to quicken. What was she doing here, with this boy, telling him her darkest secrets? How could she trust him when she knew he'd do anything the school board told him? Maybe someone, somewhere, had seen her, followed her, knew what books she was trying to find. He watched her, and although he seemed caring at first, the more she scrambled to respond to the question the more suspicious his expression became.

"It wasn't anything, really," she finally said. "Just... sickness. Sorry, the memory of her is really upsetting, you know?"

Tarven didn't look the least bit convinced. She was lying through her teeth and he knew it.

"What about you?" she asked, putting on what her dad had said was her most attractive smile. "Your parents?"

Tarven was getting ready to respond, still looking suspicious, when Andie saw Raesh and his friends come in. Her hand came up before she'd even made the decision and she hoped desperately that they would see her. Raesh spotted her almost instantly. As he and his friends started toward her, she almost collapsed under the sheer relief. But as Raesh and his friends drew near, they seemed to see something they either didn't like or, based on some unspoken principle, couldn't tolerate. They walked right by Andie, merely nodding at her, and sat at the other end of the bar.

"You know those guys?" Tarven asked, a look of disgust passing his eyes.

"I thought I did," Andie said, actually offended.

"Don't take it the wrong way. It had nothing to do with you. Them and us... We just don't mix. My friends and I don't hang out with lowlifes."

Andie was taken aback, but in the interest of preserving what seemed to have become a fragile peace in the bar, she just nodded.

"Oh. I see," she said, grabbing her purse. "It's been a fun night, Tarven. Thanks for inviting me. I guess I should get back to my place and study."

"You sure?" he asked, though it seemed more out of politeness than genuine desire for her to stay.

"Yeah. See you in school."

She left, trying not to run at top speed. On her way home, all she could think about was how hurt Raesh had looked to see her with Tarven.

CHAPTER TEN

ANDIE WOKE UP COVERED IN SWEAT. THE BED WAS floating in midair and the walls were totally engulfed in purple flames. With a fluid swipe of her hand she extinguished the flames and the bed came back down gently. She'd had a nightmare. The same nightmare she'd been having for years, only a little clearer. It had been the same voices, same people calling for help, but that time the images had improved some. She'd seen a face, the first face she'd ever seen in that show of horrors. Even now that she was awake, the voices still echoed in her head, softer than shrieks and harder than whispers, the caustic noise of terror.

She felt different. She looked at the hair falling over her shoulder. It was purple. She could guess that her eyes had probably changed, too, to their natural, vivid byzantium. Her heart raced as she looked around the room to make sure no one could see. Pressing her hand against her chest, she let out a slow, deep breath to calm her nerves. She had locked the door, there was no chance that anyone had seen. Her heart rate slowed somewhat. She used her magic to hide herself again, muttering an incantation to help keep a lid on her magic. She ran her hands through her hair and inspected it closely as she twirled the long locks between her fingers. A dark brunette. Classic, simple, unassuming. She let out a sigh of relief.

The magic flames had left no marks on the wall, though the room was as hot as an oven. The heat, of course, felt good. Fire was nourishment to a true dragonborn like Andie. At that moment, she was beyond grateful for Carmen showing her how to manipulate her icon, otherwise her life would have been over. The thought of it made her think of her mother and she looked over at her picture on the nightstand.

"What should I do?" she asked. Andie was so conflicted. Determined to find out more about her persecuted ancestors and war-ravaged heritage, she didn't know what to believe anymore. She stared longingly at her mother's photo and then fell back into the bed with an aggravated sigh.

Try as she might, Andie couldn't get back to sleep. After an hour of simply laying there, she got up and decided to go through the books she'd found in the archive. It was probably best to get them back soon before anyone could notice they were not only gone, but stolen. The books were ancient, full of dust that was nearly black, and the binding was barely managing to hold on to the pages. Those books were probably almost as old as Arvall itself. It wasn't until she was there in bed that she realized most of the books were in a different language.

She spoke three languages, but she didn't recognize that one. She'd picked them up because their titles or opening pages all made some mention of dragons, which was apparently the same word in that language as it was in her own, but the lighting had been so bad and she had been in such a hurry that she hadn't even noticed the strange characters of the alphabets. She couldn't make any sense of them. More still, she noticed that some of the books actually changed languages whenever she closed their covers; she'd be looking at one foreign language, close the book, open it again, and be looking at another. One book wouldn't open at all.

"What could be so bad that they'd go through this much trouble? Why not just throw the books away altogether?" Her questions echoed in her silent room, unanswered.

She knew that unless she could find a translator and a way to break the spells, she'd never discover the secrets of those texts. She'd become a thief for nothing. But she still had one option left. She could go back to Leabherlann, back to that doorway in the archives where she heard the voices. She was courting trouble to go back, and not only trouble, but expulsion, too. Still, she had to. If she couldn't know about dragons, she would at least know what was behind that door. She would learn what the voices were and where they came from.

Outside, the sun was finally rising. It wasn't long before Andie was dressed, fed, and on her way back to the University. The city streets seemed to admonish her for her boldness, warn her of the potential danger, but she couldn't stop. She was tired of being denied the answers to her past and her present. Tired of being denied the truth.

Because it was still early morning, the streets were clear, which gave her the solitude and quiet to clear her head in the fresh air. She checked her phone and saw messages from Raesh. She ignored them, not knowing if she owed him an explanation or not.

Either way, she had no time for his jealousy that morning.

CHAPTER ELEVEN

IT TOOK HER MOST OF THE MORNING TO ARRIVE. SHE walked as far as she could before taking the train, and the only explanation she could give herself as to why she'd walked so far without need was that she knew she was beginning to push her luck. She'd turned down her icon and gotten fairly good at sneaking around, but she knew someone would catch her if she wasn't careful. Soon enough, she found herself on campus. She'd entered the doors and hardly walked the hall when she ran into Tarven.

"Andie. What are you doing here so early?"

The unexpected encounter left her flustered. She took a moment to collect her thoughts before she spoke. "Just… wanted to get an early start."

"Early start for what? Classes don't begin for

another few hours." His eyebrow was raised in a quizzical arch as he watched her try and explain herself.

"Not that I need to explain my every whereabouts to you, Tarven, but I just wanted to finish my homework and do some studying for midterms. It's only a matter of weeks now." She crossed her arms and looked up at him, determination set on her face.

She was amazed at herself, the ease with which she'd lied and the poise she'd had while doing it. She'd been rehearsing a cover story all the way up the mountain.

"Very true," he said, suddenly breaking into a smile. "However, I think maybe your time would be better spent this morning if you skipped."

"I'm sorry, what?"

"Skip your studying and your homework. Come hang out with me for a bit. I don't want to be too on the nose, but you don't really seem to have a ton of friends. I only mention that to say that every time I see you, you're either in Leabherlann or studying in some corner. I'm sure you'll do fine on midterms. What do you say?"

She didn't want to admit it, but she was getting butterflies. She actually wanted to hang out with Tarven, talk to him, laugh with him, not to mention she hadn't missed what he said about Leabherlann. Clearly, he was watching her closer than she thought. The last thing she needed was him getting suspicious and then going back to the school board. Even if they couldn't prove she'd been in the archives, she'd be in all kinds of trouble once they found out her icon had been muted for weeks. She knew what she had to do, for now.

"Um... sure," she said. "I'd love to."

She was being sincere. It turned out not to be that much of a sacrifice after all, though it was still against her better judgement. For a moment, she *did* wonder. Why was a guy like Tarven interested in a girl like her?

She shook her head as she followed him, forcing all thoughts of her interest in Tarven from her mind. She had more important things to worry about than some stupid boy.

"Okay," he said. "I just need to pick up some things for my own studying and then we can go."

He led her through the halls and into the Academy. They went to the west-most wing and into the section of the Academy that housed the main offices for plant studies and hortological magic.

"So," Andie began, having decided to probe the waters. "You remember finding me down in the archives?"

"Staring at a door? Yep."

"Well, I was just wondering... what's actually down there? I mean, I read a couple of the plaques, but I was still kind of confused."

"It's nothing. Just another storage room. There's nothing down there except old books that aren't any good to anyone."

"How old?"

"What?"

"How old are those books? If they go back far enough they might have some interesting stuff in them. For my history class, I mean."

"Huh," he said, nonchalant. "Nah, nothing like that. Just old dusty books that need to be thrown out, is all. Nothing that hasn't already been replaced with new. You'll find the same books in the actual library."

They continued walking and Andie contemplated what he said. She knew it to be false, but she pretended to go along with it.

"Yeah, you're probably right."

"When I found you down there, you said something about voices, like there were other people down there, but that was impossible. The archive has a register for all visitors and there were no names on it that day."

"You remember the exact page from the register from that specific day weeks ago?"

"Yeah."

His voice had changed. He was on to her, just like she was on to him. She didn't know if he wanted her to stop prodding for her own sake or for his. He sighed a little and spoke gently again.

"You didn't hear anything, Andie. It was just your imagination."

He seemed so genuine that for a moment she wondered if she truly had imagined it all. Like Raesh and Carmen had said, she was under a lot of pressure that day and the archives did have a weird vibe to them. Could she be crazy? Maybe what her professor had been saying about the dragonborn was right: maybe there *was* something wrong with their blood.

That thought hurt her, though, that she was like them and they may have been a demented and terrible race. If it were true, it meant she had inherited a broken mind and her entire life was futile. Maybe she really was losing it.

When they reached the offices, Andie waited in one of the empty ones while Tarven got his things. While she was leaning against the wall, she noticed a cabinet with names. Out of simple curiosity, she leaned over to take a closer look and nearly fell over when she noticed her own name. She reached out to take the file and saw that her father's name was behind hers. Now totally obsessed, she snatched both folders from the cabinet and opened them.

"What the hell?" Her voice came out a whisper, but it echoed in the room all around her. Andie looked around the room to make sure no one had heard, and turned her attention back to the folders.

Inside was information about her father's accident, that mysterious and terrible thing that had crippled him and changed the course of their lives forever. As she read on and looked at the various photos of the aftermath, she began to notice that it wasn't adding up.

What was in that folder didn't match what she'd been told while growing up. It didn't match anything she'd ever heard about what happened. If what was in the file was true, then it hadn't been an accident at all, and the University had a hand in it. There were pictures of men in suits and the designation under them read "Searchers."

It had been many years since she'd seen one, but she could never forget them. After all, they were the only ones in the entire region allowed to carry guns—the machines that fed off of their holder's magic. Guns were the most dangerous and feared things since dragons; not only were they powered by the holder's magic, they were also fueled by that person's rage and hate. What happened when the trigger was pulled depended on the power and evil of the shooter.

The file also had several names, some of whom Andie knew were prominent politicians and high ranking officials. There were also several mentions of Taline, Arvall's rival to the north, but in all the information, she still couldn't figure out what happened.

At that point, she heard Tarven coming and nearly dropped the folders. She put all the papers and pictures back in order and only just managed to slip them back into their places in the cabinet when he appeared in the doorway.

"Come on, let's get lunch," he said. "There's no telling what you'll get up to if you're left alone."

CHAPTER TWELVE

DAYS PASSED. ANDIE HAD GROWN MORE ANXIOUS AND more frustrated. In all the days since she'd made up her mind to sneak into Leabherlann, she hadn't been able to discover anything. A group of professors were visiting the University for research and they had been in the archives from before the school opened to after it closed, giving her no opportunity to go back there. She'd had even less luck with getting back to the offices where the files were, because there was no good reason for her to even be in that wing. Her patience was wearing thin and her mind was wearing out.

That day she was hanging out with Raesh in the restaurant. It had been a while since they'd really had a chance to talk and he'd been different with her ever since he saw her with Tarven. Andie didn't like that he felt he had a right to judge, but in his defense, she had been spending a lot of time with Tarven lately.

"I'm glad you could find the time," Raesh said.

As jealous as she knew he was, there was no hint of anger or contempt in his voice. He was honestly glad to see her.

"Me, too. I feel like things have been kind of weird with us lately. Which sucks because I miss hanging out with you and Carmen."

"Well, my cousin's a firecracker. Good luck getting her to stay anywhere. As for me... well, I'm sorry I've been avoiding you. I was being a world-class jerk, but I'm ready to make up for it if you can forgive me."

"There's nothing to forgive," Andie said, smiling. "Wait, does this mean you're going to be your usual overwhelmingly annoying and flirty self again?" She winked at him as she said it, obviously poking fun at him. Perhaps even flirting a little bit, herself.

"Undoubtedly."

They smiled and just like that the past few days were erased. Whatever he might feel about her or the company she kept, Raesh was proving to be a great friend.

"So, what have you been up to?" Andie asked.

"Helping out around the restaurant, going to the movies with Carmen, working out. The usual. And reading some really cool books, too."

"You read an unhealthy number of books. And they're huge. Regular people don't read that much."

"Regular people aren't smarter than most of their teachers. Magic is your power, books are mine. If you describe to me what it's like to cast a spell, I bet it'll be pretty close to what it's like to find a truly great book."

"That's really cool, Raesh. I never knew you were this passionate. You ever think of writing one?"

"I did. Two of them actually."

"You're kidding," she said, sitting up straight in disbelief. "Where are they?"

"Collecting dust in the attic. Maybe I'll get them published someday."

"You're kind of amazing right now. And here I thought you were just an incorrigible flirt."

"Only when I'm near a girl who's worth it."

He gave her that same warm look that had won her over the first night.

"Have I told you how stunning you look in yellow?"

"Easy, boy."

"Sorry. You're just kind of perfect," he said, without flair, as if it were the simplest truth of all.

"Thank you, Raesh," she said, resisting the urge to touch his hand. She could feel a blush creep up in her cheeks, and she turned away so that he couldn't see. The last thing she needed was Raesh thinking that she was interested. "Now, for the real reason we came. Help with my magic."

"Right. I'm ready. I closed down the restaurant a bit early so we'd have the place to ourselves."

They stood and walked to the middle of the room. Andie held up her palm and manipulated the icon the way Carmen had taught her. The golden light in the center of her palm dimmed. With a wave of her hand she pushed all the tables and chairs away from them. Raesh grabbed the student grimoire and began reading off the difficult spells Andie had marked for practice. She practiced them quickly and with a growing skill she was becoming proud of. She still needed some work on the fluidity of her movements, though. Her professor said she lacked the grace that came with total confidence, but she had improved at a steady rate and her dragon magic hadn't slipped in once since the morning she woke with the walls on fire.

She almost got Raesh once, while practicing an immobility charm. Luckily it was on his left leg and they both had a good laugh when he tumbled over. They were having fun and Andie was even flirting with him a little.

"You're kind of gorgeous when you go full sorceress," Raesh said.

"You're kind of hot when you fall flat on your face."

"Does that mean you like the view of me from behind?"

"Neither view is so bad."

After they'd finished, they sat down again. Andie

was feeling more confident now that she and Raesh were back on good terms, and she wanted to tell him about the files she found in the offices. She waited until he wasn't distracted and explained everything that had happened, up until Tarven had come back into the room. When she finished telling him everything she'd seen and read, he needed a moment to process.

"Andie, my first instinct is to ask you how you were feeling that day. I mean, are you sure you saw what you think you saw? If you say that it's there, then I want to believe you, but that's a huge accusation. Are you sure you didn't misread it?"

"I remember it as clear as day. It was a file on me and one on my father. I didn't have time to look in mine, but I went through most of his. I know what I saw. And I was feeling fine that day. I was a little frustrated, sure, but I'm always a little frustrated. It doesn't mean I'm crazy."

"Of course not. I would never suggest that. But if what you say is true, then this is big. Maybe too big for us. I'm trying to make sense of it. The University having something to do with your father's accident? I can't even imagine what it would mean for-"

The bell on the door rang and Andie turned around to see Tarven.

"Oh, I completely forgot." She waved to him as he approached and she could hear Raesh huff behind her.

But when she turned around he was at least trying to smile. He was a good friend.

"Hey," Tarven said to Andie, ignoring Raesh completely. "You ready to go?"

"Sure," she said, feeling uncomfortable to be literally and figuratively between them.

She stood and began to gather her things. She was having so much fun with Raesh, but she'd already made plans with Tarven and, somehow, she just felt she couldn't give up the opportunity.

"Alright, I'm all set," she said. "I don't think you've met my friend Raesh. He's really great."

She emphasized the "great" and winked at Raesh. His smile then could have lit the night. Tarven mumbled something which might have been a greeting or a curse and then he turned to leave. Andie gave Raesh a hug and left, trying not to notice the disappointment on his face.

AFTER SPENDING some time just hanging out together and chatting, they arrived at the University's Victory garden. Tarven was working on a special project that he wanted Andie's help with. They were working diligently, laughing and joking as they went along, when somehow the conversation managed to turn around to Andie's dad again.

She became vague with her answers, even a bit defensive at one point, but the butterflies inside her kept her from getting outright angry with Tarven. Maybe he was just a curious guy. Maybe he just wanted to know her better.

"So, your dad must really miss you," he said.

"Yeah. I miss him, too. We were always together before I came here. It's like losing a piece of myself. But, luckily, I'm a little ahead in my work and I think I'll be able to go home for a visit soon. Anything you want me to ask him, since you seem so keen on knowing everything about him?" She asked playfully, trying to lighten the mood and let him know she wasn't upset. He seemed to understand.

"Ask him how he raised such an amazing young woman," he said, smiling at her so beautifully that she had to catch her breath. "And ask him about his time on the council. That must have been spectacular."

The last statement made Andie pause. She'd never told Tarven her dad was on Taline's council. She'd never told anyone.

"What did you say?" she asked. "How did you know my dad was on the council?"

"Huh? Oh, you told me, remember?"

"No," she said, dropping her tools and turning to face him. "I didn't. That's not something I would talk about with anybody, ever. How did you know?"

"You must have told me," he maintained, failing to

meet her eyes. "Or it must have slipped out. Come on, we have to get this finished before-"

"Tarven, why aren't you looking at me? How did you know my dad was on the council? Who told you? What else do you know?"

"Look, Andie," he said, finally putting his tools down, but still not facing her. "You got drunk that night at the bar, okay? You were spilling all of your secrets and this thing about your dad was one of them. I don't 'know' anything, alright? Only what you told me."

She just watched him for a moment. He couldn't look at her. It told her everything she needed to know.

"I'm feeling sick," she said, taking off her apron and tossing it aside.

She left without another word.

CHAPTER THIRTEEN

A COUPLE DAYS LATER, ANDIE HAD CALMED SOME. She'd talked things over with Marvo and decided that Tarven couldn't possibly be a spy. Marvo wouldn't let Andie know everything he knew about the University and the things it had set in motion over time, but he said as far as he knew they didn't operate like that anymore.

Andie spent some time away from Tarven, but somehow worked herself up to trusting him again, or at least wanting to trust him. If she was being honest with herself, she knew that she should stay away from him and that something wasn't right; she knew in her bones that Tarven knew more than he was letting on and that he was either up to something or knew someone who was, but she really liked him. And she believed that deep down he truly was the honest guy she thought she knew. She couldn't blame him for wanting to know more about her and her family. She was just as curious about him.

That day, she was sitting behind Carmen and Yara. When Andie registered for classes, she had decided to enroll in one class that was several stages ahead of a first-year course load. Luckily, Theory of Temporal Incantations had no prerequisites. So far, Andie had fallen somewhat behind, but the subject matter was finally starting to come together for her. Carmen and Yara were talking excitedly between themselves about the upcoming One Thousandth Winter Festival—it was actually the one thousandth and first festival, but the festival had been suspended the previous year due to concerns about an ancient curse that was supposed to manifest in the year 1,000. Of course, nothing happened, but it made for a good story. They chattered away while Professor Harrock proselytized about space-time meditation and inter-dimensional spell casting.

As it happened, Tarven had recently become Professor Harrock's teaching assistant and, at the moment, he was sitting in a corner, behind and to the left of the professor, distracting Andie with a staring contest. His eyes were almost talking, taunting, teasing her with their depth and attraction. They'd been at this game for nearly the entire class. He'd win, then she'd win, then he'd win again. They were having so much fun that they'd completely let reality and time slip away. That was especially dangerous for Andie, because she'd become so comfortable there, watching him, that she let her dragon magic slip out of her control.

She was so immersed in the moment that she was being consumed by the thought of Tarven. His eyes. His lips. The way he laughed and the way he turned in the sunlight. Her concealment spell had already begun fading before she noticed. By pure luck, she happened to look down at her arm and see that the hairs there were turning a light, but radiant purple. She sat up as straight as a beam and closed her eyes to focus on repressing the magic. After that, she turned her attention away from Tarven, sending him one last smile.

She tried to pay attention to Professor Harrock, but she had missed too much of the lecture and she had no idea what the "paradigm shift of the temporal grimoire anomaly" was. Carmen and Yara were still chatting away, so Andie leaned forward to talk with them.

"So, I've been eavesdropping and I'm kind of interested in this Winter Festival business," she said. "Want to fill me in?"

"Oʜ, so you mean you're done ogling Tarven?"

Carmen never beat around the bush; she spoke her mind unflinchingly. Andie knew she was only kidding with her, but still there was something almost bitter about it, something strangely cold. Andie had been suspecting for a while now that Carmen resented her a little for not dating Raesh. Or maybe Carmen wanted Tarven. That was most likely the reason.

"Well, yeah," Andie said. "Sorry, couldn't help it."

"Don't apologize to me," Yara said. "That is one fantastic looking specimen. I'm kind of jealous actually."

"The world is full of great guys and I know you'll find one someday," Andie said. "Now, tell me about the festival."

"Well, it was supposed to have been held last year, but they thought a bunch of people were going to die and evil was going to rise, so on and so forth. Long story short, it's the festival's thousandth year and they're saying it's going to be the biggest celebration Noelle's ever seen. They want to make the millennial an occasion that will never be forgotten."

"Usually, they expect tens of thousands to come," Carmen said. "But this year they're expecting millions. It's going to be the most spectacular thing of our lives. Can you imagine even being alive for this? Hundreds of years from now they'll still be talking about this."

"Sounds exciting," Andie said.

"Have you never heard of the Winter Festival?"

"Sure. My dad always told me it was a really big deal in Arvall, but we never came because he said that people came in from all over Noelle and it could be potentially dangerous."

"Andie, take it from me," Carmen said, leaning in. "There is nothing like the Winter Festival anywhere in this region or even this hemisphere. It's primarily for the University and its students, but over the centuries the whole city began to take part. You have no idea what you're in for. Ball gowns, dancing, food, music, exhibitions of creatures brought from distant lands, magic you can't even imagine..."

Carmen trailed off as she noticed that Andie was once again flirting with Tarven. In her defense, Andie hadn't even noticed that she'd stopped listening.

"Andie. Andie!"

Andie snapped back into her body, her eyes landing on Carmen.

"Oh, I'm so sorry, Carmen, I didn't even know what was going on. That was rude of me."

"Are you going to go to the festival with him?"

Andie couldn't tell how Carmen meant the question: was it an accusation or a hint into her disappointment? Both? Andie became flustered and could feel her cheeks begin to burn as they reddened. Suddenly she was nervous.

"I don't see why not," she said. "If he wants to ask me."

She honestly didn't know if he did.

ANDIE CAUGHT SKY 6 on her way home after class.

She suddenly had a lot to think about, namely how her relationship—if she could even call it that—with Tarven was going to affect her relationship with her host family. Marvo, Raesh, and Carmen had been nothing but good to her and had helped her through some incredibly tough times. They were still helping her with the transition from Michaelson to Arvall City, and from taking care of her father to taking care of herself. She didn't want to seem uncaring and she didn't want them to think of her as someone who had toyed with Raesh's feelings. Though she was beginning to suspect that she had, inadvertently. What would happen if they thought she'd chosen Tarven over them? She didn't know what she would do without them.

Andie had tried to get Tarven to socialize with them, but he simply wouldn't deign to talk to Marvo and Raesh. He had no problems talking to Carmen, though, since she had magic in her blood, but he had no patience and no respect for nomags. Raesh had made an honest attempt to compromise and meet Tarven halfway, but it hadn't worked. Tarven's elitist priorities were ingrained in him. It was his greatest flaw that Andie resented, but she forced herself to see past it, through to the good in him.

Marvo was doing his very best to pretend that

Tarven didn't bother him and he didn't mind having him around. Carmen seemed too torn to make up her mind either way; she'd gotten by this far by simply avoiding the topic. But Raesh had been a complete sweetheart and a terrific friend. He seemed to understand that Andie, for whatever reason, had chosen Tarven and that he, Raesh, now had to do what any good friend should and be happy for her. And he was. Certainly, he didn't pretend to like Tarven and he'd stopped trying to greet him, but he stayed courteous through it all.

SKY 6 sped down the mountain as if furious with the world. Outside the window, the rain came in torrents. Sometime during the Fifth Cycle of the First Age the sky had changed. Some say it was because of the massive and horrific war that had spread over the earth, others say it was because of the sky being stained by the blood of the Cloud Mages as their species went extinct by the millions. Some say it was simply time. But since then, the lighting had turned green and more violent than at any other time in the history of the earth.

Arvall City was protected by powerful charms and incantations, but there were whole regions in Noelle that had been rendered uninhabitable because the lightning struck the earth with such ferocity and frequency. At the Hot Salts of Mithraldia, the lightning struck the earth some seven thousand times per hour when it rained. Now when a storm came, the world beneath flashed in green bursts of swift and violent light, like some great deity in the sky above had gone mad. Even the rain had changed over time, and if you looked closely you could see the hint of green in the drops. The spellglass had been transformed into a striated pattern with raised wavelike ridges in order to help the rain roll off easier. Andie watched the drops leaving the window almost as soon as they landed. Her mind drifted and she started thinking of her past.

THAT NIGHT they'd come to Michaelson to check for dragonborn descendants. There had been an attack in Taline earlier that day and the council of the city had contacted the University and asked for the Searchers. The Searchers were essentially just mercenaries, but no one questioned the University. By the time her parents finally got home from Taline, the Searchers were already pounding on the door and Andie was alone. Her mom and dad fought off the first wave of men valiantly; Andie could still remember their strength and power, the beautiful and mesmerizing way they used their magic to defend her. A beautiful and terrifying blend of dragon and sorcerer. Her family had run outside to escape, but they were caught in matrices, magical traps set up to stop magical beings from teleporting. The Searchers took her mom away and Andie never saw her again. They nearly killed her dad. They tried to erase their memory of her mother, but Andie's concealed dragon blood magic had protected their minds.

SOMETIMES, Andie wished her magic hadn't seeped out, hadn't protected all those memories of her mother. She could have grown up so much happier, so much more whole if she didn't always carry with her the terrible memories of that night. It definitely would have saved her father unimaginable pain and grief. So many things could have been different.

When she finally made it to the restaurant, she'd managed to clear her head while walking through the city streets. She was ready to get to her daily tasks. Marvo and Raesh never stopped insisting that she didn't need to earn her keep, but she wouldn't hear of it. Besides, she knew they'd grown to like her company. She came in and said hi to them both, immediately getting to work. Raesh was cleaning tables and Andie worked on the floors, but she kept getting distracted. Raesh was joking with her about the way she mopped and she was trying her best to focus on what he was saying, but she couldn't stop thinking about the Winter Festival and what it would mean to be asked to it by Tarven.

"You know, mopping is supposed to have a sort of rhythm," he teased.

Andie made no reply, having not heard him because of her deep reverie.

"Well," Raesh continued, not to be daunted. "If you can't move a mop, you probably can't move your feet either. In my experience, a girl who can't find a rhythm in her daily life certainly isn't going to pick it up overnight for a dance."

"Yeah, probably will," Andie said. She had no idea what she was replying to or even what she was saying.

She'd been mopping the same small circle for nearly five minutes, and while she was clueless, Raesh had noticed. He had also guessed, correctly, that it was probably Tarven she was thinking about. But if she'd been paying attention, she would've seen the intense resolve on Raesh's face. He'd started and now he had to finish.

"And to think, I was going to ask you to the Winter Festival," he said, finishing with a brave smile when he must have been terrified.

"Do you think Tarven will ask me to the Winter Festival? Should I ask him?"

She hadn't heard a single word he'd said.

"You know, why don't you call it a day," he said, his face looking crushed and angry. "I can manage the rest of this."

"Raesh, I'm not going to let you clean all of this on your own. Let me-"

"I said go, Andie!"

As soon as he said it his expression changed. He seemed surprised and even ashamed at himself for yelling. Still, with a last lingering look he turned his back on Andie and went into the kitchen. Andie was oblivious, having missed the entire conversation only to catch the ending rage. She leaned the mop against the wall and went up to her room, totally confused.

CHAPTER FOURTEEN

ANDIE WAS HARDLY IN HER BED FIVE MINUTES BEFORE she decided to go to Leabherlann. She made up her mind to study and engage in yet another futile search for texts on the dragonborn or anything relating to dragons at all.

When she reached the great library, Carmen was there. She was flirting—incredibly shamelessly—with Fohrn, the young green-eyed assistant who was filling in while Murakami was out sick. Fohrn was sweet and although he wasn't stupid, he was rather soft and could be persuaded to allow almost anything for the promise of friendship or romantic attention. He was the worst possible person for the job. Andie sat at a quiet table a few rows ahead of Carmen and waited, knowing Carmen would either see her or get tired of Fohrn and leave, having to pass Andie to do it. It didn't take long. Carmen seemed engrossed in whatever Fohrn was talking about, but she happened to look Andie's way and caught her eye. She excused herself and came over to Andie's table.

"So, I heard Tarven might be asking you to the dance," she said.

Andie opened her mouth to reply, but then closed it. Things with Tarven were constantly up and down, but lately they'd been relatively good. The only problem was Raesh, who, first, had feelings that couldn't be ignored, second, was a really good friend and had made every effort to be happy for Andie and get to know Tarven, and third, was Carmen's cousin. When Carmen asked Andie why she was so upset, Andie told her all of this and about what had happened at the restaurant.

"He was just so angry," Andie finished.

"Andie," Carmen began, touching her hand. "I know you care about Raesh and I know he's your best friend, but I don't think you really appreciate how he feels."

"Carmen, I know Raesh likes me, bu—"

"Raesh loves you. He's in love with you, Andie. All that flirting and nonchalance he puts on is just an act, and it's not even a good one anymore. You're a gifted sorceress, brilliant even, and you have a way and a rapport with magic that I can't begin to fathom, but you're not so good at small details. You don't notice things. Like how Raesh shifted his entire weekly schedule just so he could be with you when you work. Or how he follows you in the mornings to make sure you make it to the train safely. You don't even know that most of the time he's the one who cooks your food, not Uncle Marvo. Did you know that when we first met I didn't even like you?"

"What? Why not?"

"It doesn't matter. What matters is that it was Raesh who made me promise to stick with you. He wanted me to teach you, protect you. He's what brought us together. He's been working in the background of your life since you first got into Arvall."

And without any delay or deliberation, Andie began to understand. Truly understand. She was starting to see Raesh for the first time and it was no wonder he'd been so mad. How could she have been so blind for so long? His reaction had been so intense because his feelings were. And, strangest of all, Andie wasn't sorry he felt that way.

"That being said, nothing excuses his temper," Carmen said, regaining her composure. "Knowing Raesh, he'll be waiting for you to come back so he can apologize. It might do you some good to apologize, too."

Andie mumbled something, but didn't put up much resistance to the idea. They both knew Carmen was right. Raesh would eventually have to accept the way things were, but other than acknowledging Raesh's feelings in her own mind, Andie hadn't done much in the way of protecting him. She sat with Carmen for as long as she could stand, until the guilt became too much and she had to go.

She got up, claiming she was going to look for some books, but really, she just wanted to message Raesh from somewhere private. Even though Carmen wouldn't have been able to know what Andie was sending, it still felt weird to have someone else's eyes on her while she dealt with Raesh. "Dealt with" because there was simply no other way to put it without verbose circumvention. She found a quiet, empty corner and sat on the oak and lamb armchair, her back against the warm, smooth surface.

Raesh... It's been weird with us lately. Not my intention. Still a chance for us?

"Great," she mumbled to herself. "Now I've become those people who can't even be bothered to make full sentences. City life does not suit me."

A chance? he responded.

She knocked her head against the high back of the armchair. She'd used the wrong language. She'd led him on again. She took a breath and tried again, wondering when she'd finally break the cycle, finally allow Raesh to have just a modicum of respect.

To be real friends. She wrote. *REAL friends. I know*

me being with Tarven is hard for you. I'm sorry. Can you believe that?

It seemed a terrifyingly long wait until he responded and Andie had nearly given up hope that he would.

Sure. To both. I'm trying as hard as I can to just be happy for you Andie. TOUGH. But you're worth having in my life. One way or another. If friends is the only option, I'll take it.

Me, too. Best friends. Want to come hang out at magic school?

Try to stop me. An hour good?

Great. See you soon.

Feeling perhaps a thousand times better, Andie got up and was off again to look for more books. Without even wasting time on the thought of checking the public areas, Andie headed straight for the archives on the lower levels. She skipped right down into the hallway leading to the archives, brimming with the excitement of mending her friendship with Raesh, when she saw Tarven and Professor Harrock standing in the entrance to the archives at the end of the hall. She hid in a small indentation of the wall that was barely as wide as she was.

Tarven and the professor were arguing in rough whispers, checking over their shoulders, and very nearly trembling with the force of whatever emotion was animating them. Andie tried her best to listen to them, but they were just far enough from her to be inaudible.

She thought she might hear something about added security, maybe something about concealment spells, but just when their conversation was rising to a decipherable level, her phone buzzed. Knowing they'd be turning around to track the sound, Andie took off.

CHAPTER FIFTEEN

LATER THAT EVENING, RAESH MET ANDIE ON CAMPUS. They opted for a walk in front of the University's façade, the long side of the building facing the direction of Arvall.

"So, how's school been going?" Raesh asked, genuinely eager to mend ties. "I know you said your professor in your history class was a... what was it... dragon hating muckmouth?"

"I don't think I said 'muckmouth.'"

"You did. There's no way I'd make that up."

"Well, at least you know which class is my least favorite. I don't even know why the board is so upset with him. Everything he's saying falls right in line with Arvall's treatment of dragon and dragonborn history. All of Noelle's treatment. He literally hasn't said a single kind thing or mentioned even one useful contribution dragons made during their time. I can't believe they were all so bad. No race is perfect, but... I just won't believe it."

"Don't slap me, but do you think, even in the smallest, darkest parts of yourself, that he might be right? That the whole world might be right?"

Andie hesitated, not wanting to admit the truth, but knowing her friendship with Raesh couldn't be built on things kept back from each other.

"Sometimes. But if that's true then... it would just be too horrible, wouldn't it? An entire race persecuted and killed because of the belief that they are evil. If there's even the slightest chance that we are wrong. That they weren't these awful, evil things, then their entire race's massacre has been covered by a lie. Does that not make you wonder?"

"I guess so. But Andie, it's in the past. There are no more dragons and probably no more dragonborn people in the world anymore. It's not really relevant, which is probably why the University is angry with your professor."

"Ugh. Enough about muckmouth..."

Raesh laughed. Andie tried to keep a straight face.

"... it's a shame you can't come in the University. Nomags aren't allowed inside, but I'd love to show you around."

Raesh stopped walking. He was looking down at his feet and even when Andie stopped and walked back to him, he still couldn't meet her eyes. Andie poked him playfully at first, but when he still wouldn't answer after several moments, she became worried. She grabbed him and shook him hard.

"Raesh!"

His eyes leapt up. He seemed surprised to find her holding him and himself holding her, too. His breathing seemed to be off.

"Andie, I haven't told you everything."

"What do you mean?"

"I mean I told you I was a nomag. And I was *born* a nomag, but something happened. When I was twelve, my mother died. On the day of her death she gave me something, a parting gift so that I could protect myself from the world."

"A gift?" Andie echoed, confused. "Like a protection spell or an idol?"

"Andie, have you ever heard of the Kyrian Bloom?"

"No."

"Queen Kyri was queen of Hightowyr many ages ago. Her reign was full of war, famine, misfortune, and ruin. The city nearly vanished under her watch. She was a good queen, wise and fair, but the times simply didn't favor her. Peace wasn't her destiny. Convinced that her life had brought only harm to the people she loved so much, Queen Kyri set in motion the circumstances of her own death. No one knows who helped her or who even saw it. So much has been lost to history. But the queen had a child. A daughter whom she loved undeniably. The daughter was born human, since the queen had married a human man, and the queen was scared for her. Queen Kyri created a spell, some say the most difficult and brilliant spell of all, that would allow her daughter to have magic. The spell needed so much spirit and power that the queen knew she could not survive it, but for her daughter, she did it anyway. She cast the spell, allowing the princess to have magic taken straight from the queen's blood. It worked. The queen died, but her daughter possessed her magic."

"Raesh, I think maybe you read too much," Andie laughed. "What does that have to do with you?"

"My mother did the same thing to me."

"Raesh, are you saying that-"

"I have magic. I'm a magical nomag, so to speak. A pearl-blood."

"What?" Andie asked, taking a few steps back. "I don't think I understand, Raesh. A magical nomag? Impossible. And what's a pearl-blood?"

"Have you ever seen a pearl? The way the colors on the surface of it are beautiful, but come in and out as you turn the pearl, dancing or skipping like a creek? Pearl-bloods can harness magic, but it's incredibly temperamental and even unstable. It's unreliable. Dangerous. It might lift a stone or it might lift a village, it's never consistent enough to tell, as we don't have the natural-born ability to control it."

Andie took a minute to let this in, a minute more to truly bask in the revelation. Could she have heard this right? Then she smiled.

"Raesh, you're a sorcerer," she said, throwing her arms around him. "This is incredible."

"Yeah," Raesh said hesitantly, warming to the excitement by watching Andie. "Yeah, I guess it is."

"It's amazing."

"Well, actually," Raesh paused. "Not a sorcerer. Not really. I wasn't born into the magic, so it's not really something I can go around flaunting, you know? It's not exactly viewed as favorable, if you know what I mean. The University would never let me in knowingly. They don't consider us to be true magic wielders."

Andie shook her head. "Incredible. I didn't even know such a thing existed. Magical nomags. I wouldn't believe it if I didn't already know you were incapable of lying…"

A red blush crept up on Raesh's cheeks as he ran his hand through his hair. "Yeah. Incredible, I guess is the word."

"You're a jerk for lying to me, though," she said, punching him in the arm. "I've kind of been feeling sorry for you, for no reason at all, it turns out. I can't believe you didn't tell me, I can't believe Carmen didn't tell me!"

"She doesn't know. Nobody knows, not even my

dad. Pearl magic is unpredictable Andie. I don't deny that my mother gave me a gift, but this is a hard thing."

"No one else knows? How have you managed to keep this a secret this whole time, Raesh?"

Raesh shrugged. "Self-preservation, I guess."

Okay. I get that. But how did she do it?"

"Well, she was dying anyway. She just wanted to keep watching over me. The Kyrian Bloom only works on a person who has no magic but direct magical ancestry through the mother or father."

"That's incredible, Raesh. It must be hard."

"There are worse things, I suppose."

"Yeah. Well, you say it's too bad I can't go to the University, but now you can see it's pretty complicated. But maybe I should show you."

He grabbed her hand and rushed toward the front doors. They entered the University and went down the long entrance hall. When they reached the heart of the mountain, Raesh took Andie down the hallway to the far left, the one Carmen had shown her, but avoided. Above them, the Mountain Faeries were moving slower, finishing their deliveries for the day and drifting up and off into the mountain in small droves. On and on Raesh went, pulling Andie along behind him, until they were suddenly in a very old part of the University. Judging by the size and shape of the buildings there, it was the old faculty dormitories from the school's first opening. It didn't seem as if it had been updated in centuries. No one seemed to even be cleaning it.

"Raesh," Andie gasped, when he finally stopped, "How do you know the University so well? I thought you'd never been here before?"

"That was lie number two. Sorry. I actually went here, a few years back. It wasn't for long, though."

"What? You were a student here. I don't…"

"Shh," Raesh interrupted her. "Keep your voice down."

"No one's here, Raesh. Your secret's safe with me." Andie put her arm around him and gave him a squeeze. "Why'd you leave? Were you afraid of what your magic could do? *Would* do?"

"That was definitely one of the reasons."

"What were the others?"

Raesh started to answer and then stopped. He just stood there, quietly looking at his shoes like he'd done outside. Then he grabbed her hand and was off again, this time leading her through the maze of abandoned buildings, around and across and through, back and seemingly down, down, down into the depths of the University. Andie found herself among gargantuan, stunning ruins, brittle and broken structures in every direction as far as her eye could see, like some great field of fallen things. They stumbled across the foundations of ancient buildings, hurried under arches that by then must have been friends of time, jumped over piles of jagged and glittering stones. Andie realized what it was. Hightowyr.

The world down there was ancient, fallen, and forgotten. Dying, yet alive. A startling and mystifying contrast to the modern majesty of the skyscrapers of Arvall.

Out of nowhere, voices rang in around them and Raesh ducked down, pulling Andie with him. They were lucky because where they were, they were hidden on three sides with the open side facing away from the voices. Andie was nervous, knowing they probably weren't allowed back there. She took a chance and peeked around the top of the pile of rubble. She could see Tarven and some of his friends she met before. They were laughing and walking around as if they owned the world. They cast spells at each other as they went, having fun. Andie exhaled in relief.

"It's just Tarven," she said to Raesh. "Come on. We can come out."

But as she tried to rise, Raesh pulled her down again. She turned to him, shocked and a little angry.

"Be quiet," Raesh said.

Andie wanted to argue, but the look on Raesh's face frightened her a little, as if he knew something—*truly* knew something. She sat back down next to him, wondering if it was simple jealousy that was making Raesh act this way. She rolled her eyes in frustration, but when she looked at Raesh again, he had gone completely pale. Immediately, she went from irritated to concerned. Yet it wasn't long before Tarven and his friends were leaving and Raesh began to relax, regaining his color. When she was sure they were all gone, she helped Raesh to his feet and waited for an explanation. When it became clear that she wasn't going to get one, she started in.

"Raesh, what happened? What was wrong?"

"Nothing. I'm fine."

"Yeah, you're fine now. What about a couple of minutes ago?"

"I don't want to... you wouldn't understand."

"Raesh, you've told me a lot tonight and I appreciate it, I truly do. But you've given me even more questions and no answers. Now I've known you to not like Tarven, be critical of him, even jealous, but never scared."

"I wasn't scared."

"Raesh, I've never seen you like that before. Just be honest with me. I tell you everything, why can't you open up?" That last bit made her pause a moment, but she shook away her worry about not actually being truly honest with him. She was as honest as she could be, without outing her true heritage. If anyone understood Raesh's explanation of self-preservation, it was Andie.

"Some things are too much, Andie."

He watched her, probably trying to figure out what questions she would ask next and how he could deflect them. He seemed much calmer and now it was Andie who was going pale. It had shaken her to her bones to see Raesh like that. Raesh, who was always so strong and so true. Raesh, who was honest, direct, and fearless.

What had happened between him and Tarven? He hadn't seemed afraid the last time he saw Tarven, and Andie couldn't think of anything about where they were that could be to blame. Was it Tarven's friends? It couldn't have been, because Raesh had seen them that night at the bar. Had something happened in the time since? Andie instinctively held her head at her temples, unnerved. Raesh simply watched and waited like a dog outside of a window, like he knew Andie could come to the right conclusion by herself.

Some moments passed. Andie decided not to press the issue. Honestly, she was afraid to know.

CHAPTER SIXTEEN

RAESH TURNED AND CONTINUED LEADING ANDIE DOWN through the ruins, only this time he didn't bother taking her hand. Something had just changed between them and even if neither of them could admit it out loud, they both knew it inside. Farther and farther they went, the mystical light above them beginning to dim some. Soon they came to a gargantuan tunnel entrance, and, though there did seem to be some light inside, it was significantly darker than where they were coming from.

Andie still couldn't believe that she'd had no idea this place even existed. All these months she had been going to this school and exploring with both Carmen and Tarven, and she had never even come close to these spaces. She wondered how Raesh could possibly know all this. He clearly knew more about the University than she did. And what was even more obvious—and what was doubtless to blame for this growing rift between them—was that he was hiding something and whatever it was must have been enormous.

Once inside the tunnel, Andie realized that it was actually a corridor, a grand corridor fashioned in the style of the earliest of ancient architecture. The corridor must have been at least as old as Hightowyr. It was dusty, dark, and the air wasn't quite clear; Andie had a sneaking suspicion that it was probably damp down there. They went a bit farther before Raesh stopped and turned to her. He smiled, seemingly not sure if it would work so soon after the episode, but Andie found herself smiling in return. It wasn't that she wanted to, but it was as if some impulse in her relationship to him had overridden her new mistrust of him.

"Look around you," Raesh said.

Andie turned and looked up at the walls of the corridor. She could see now that the walls weren't blank, and, in fact, there were colors there. The colors were incredibly old, to be sure—flaking, faded, with whole sections missing where the stone had fallen out of the foundation—but still there. She peered hard through the dimness, but couldn't make out whatever it was the walls were depicting. She raised her hand.

"*Solas*," she whispered, waving her fingers as she did so.

Instantly, the light around them was amplified and the corridor went from bleak outline to golden lit majesty. Andie could see now that the colors were massive murals. Hundreds upon hundreds of murals running the long, long length of the walls and the ceiling. Now that the light had improved, Andie could see that there was not just one corridor, but many. They were standing next to the entrance to another corridor, as grand and abandoned as that one. She could see multiple other entrances down the corridor. There must have been miles of them down there.

"I know I should have shown this to you before," Raesh said, looking everywhere except at Andie. "But I just didn't know how. And I hoped that maybe you'd find the information you were after in some other place. Some other way. This was just so... gruesome. I didn't want this to be the only source you had for your questions and your research. You deserve better, Andie."

Just as she was beginning to wonder what Raesh was talking about, she finally began to fully comprehend what it was she was seeing. The murals were beautiful, masterfully crafted, but they were violent and, in some instances, even grotesque. They depicted blood, carnage, murder, magic, and mayhem. It was the dragons and the dragonborn. It was their slaughter.

Their blood was the intermittent flash of burgundy among the characters, their heads the oblong shapes at the foot of certain helmeted figures. And the so-called pure sorcerers and sorceresses were present as well, clothed in gold and surrounded by iridescent rays of power as they towered over the fragile, dying bodies of the dragonborn. It was meant to show the glory and might of "pure" magic, but all Andie could see was unadulterated hate and a totally one-sided history. In some sections, the dragonborn were placed in vertical lines, with small branches of people shooting out in wider and wider reaches as the lines went down; it was trying to convey the systematic extermination of the descendants of the dragonborn. Genocide. There are men being impaled. One woman with blue hair and eyes tied to a post and burned alive. Children being thrown into snake pits. Andie was so shocked that she was almost choking on her terror. She'd had no idea just how involved in the purge the University had been.

"Some time ago, I don't exactly know when, the council of Arvall intervened to keep the politics against the dragonborn more neutral," Raesh began. "Or at least, that was what they told everyone. There have been rumors and whispers that they still conduct raids, even today. Whenever they hear of a dragonborn or think there may be an incidence of dragon magic, they swarm. They say that the only reason they've never been caught is because the Searchers are taught a special variant of the obliviating spell. Whole communities wiped clean of any knowledge the University was ever there or ever murdered and erased a loved one, a neighbor, a friend."

Raesh paused and looked over at Andie, likely waiting for a reaction, but she was still taking in all of the horrible stories on the wall, all the destruction. The ruined lives. Tears began falling from her eyes. Raesh continued.

"I don't know. Maybe the rumors are just rumors. Maybe the University stopped all that a long time ago. Maybe I'm paranoid. All I know is that I couldn't stand to be associated with this University or with anyone or anything that could do something so terrible. Unstable magic or not, I had to get out, Andie. I felt like I couldn't breathe in this place, like I was the one who'd done all those things and hurt all those people. I don't even remember what I was doing down here when I found these," he said, indicating the murals. "But when I saw these walls, these crimes against everything good... it was my last day as a student here. They butchered an entire race."

"Two races," Andie said, barely above a whisper. "The dragons and the dragonborn."

She turned to Raesh, tears running down her cheeks as fresh as the new hurt breaking open inside her.

"I had no idea you were such an... that you felt so strongly about it," she said.

"How could I not? I can never forget these corridors.

This pain that they smeared across the walls as some sort of celebration."

Andie then became conflicted. Here was a boy who'd become her best friend, who cared for her in so many ways on so many levels. He had been there for her every day, had made her laugh, had helped her practice her magic, had introduced her to Carmen, her other best friend. He'd brought her down here and shown her a whole new world. He'd even shared his darkest secret with her. And she wanted to do the same. She had longed for so many years to tell someone about herself, about who she was and what she could do. But Raesh was also proving how many secrets he'd kept. He'd kept his magic a secret. He'd kept these corridors from her when he knew how much she struggled to find even a hint of truth. He'd refused to tell her what had happened between him and Tarven and was probably doing so out of sheer jealousy. Yes, he'd shared a lot with her that day, but it had ultimately served to prove that she didn't really know who he was. She couldn't share anything with him, not yet, no matter how desperately she wanted to.

Not only that, but sharing her secret could put her life in danger. And her father's. Carmen. Marvo. Anyone she'd ever known and cared about. She couldn't do it. She'd have to keep waiting for that freedom, that paradise of a life when she wouldn't have to constantly emit magic just to hide her appearance every single hour of every single day. That time hadn't come yet.

Finally, she simply said, "Show me more."

Raesh took her another five or ten minutes down the corridor and then they turned right onto a different one. This corridor was much more modern and of all the spaces they'd seen, this one had unquestionably had the most upkeep. In fact, it was so recent that it showed a beautiful and sprawling glass city. Arvall. The mural couldn't possibly be too old and perhaps the entire area wasn't as old and abandoned as she'd thought. The mural went on to show a large group of dragonborn descendants. Their faces were blurred and smudged, obviously done by the artist to ensure that even as abstract representations in an underground mural they would have no autonomy, no grace in defeat. The color of their hair varied, as did the color of the smudges of their eyes. They were being publicly executed, like the vilest criminals. She didn't want to know, but she couldn't help asking.

"How long ago was this?"

She knew her mother had been taken eighteen years ago. This mural looked recent enough to have been done around that time.

"The University only *agreed*—which I use skeptically—to stop the persecution about ten years ago. But the whole city knows it was only because they believed they'd already killed the last of the dragonborn."

"I have to leave," Andie said.

Andie turned to leave and before she knew it she was running. She was running as hard and as fast as she'd ever run in her life. She ran desperately, angrily. All those murals had brought back her mother's disappearance in vivid and excruciating detail. It wasn't as if Andie could ever forget, but seeing all that senseless murder and chaos, all that wanton bloodshed, had made that night appear before Andie's eyes as if it were happening again. Her parents fighting off the strangers. The guns. The matrices. The fear and confusion. The Searchers. Her mother being dragged away. Her father lying face down in the grass. The Searchers erasing her mother from every picture in the house. The screams. They'd never known for certain that it had been the University; the raids had always been merely rumors, unproven and unfounded. But now she knew. It was the University who'd kidnapped and probably killed her mother. This place she was in, that she came to every day, was responsible for the fact that Andie could never see or hold her mother again.

She found herself heading for Leabherlann, desperate to learn something, anything. There must be something in there. She swatted at low-flying Faeries as she raced through the halls.

Why did they kill all the descendants? What could

the race possibly have done? Why were her people killed?

Raesh had yelled something at her as she began to run. It hadn't stuck at first and only then, with the distance between them and her blood pounding in her ears and her mind crystal clear from rage and pain, could she comprehend what he'd said.

"Stay out. This is a dangerous place."

CHAPTER SEVENTEEN

By the time she reached Leabherlann, Andie realized it was very late. Still, she couldn't go home then, not without at least checking a few rows for information. Some book somewhere inside that place had to have at least a partial history or tangential information about the persecution of the dragonborn descendants. All the professor ever taught in his tirades was that the dragons were tyrants and the dragonborn were evil, dark. That's all anybody ever said about them, and even that was rare because nobody really talked about them or what happened. Ever.

All she'd ever known of them was that they "must be destroyed." It had been drilled into her by everyone except her father. He'd always told her stories of warmth and compassion. He'd painted the dragons and dragonborn as kind, loyal, good. And while her mother was alive, she'd only ever given Andie love and safety. Her mother was pure dragonborn, could trace her ancestry all the way back to Gordric, one of the greatest dragons that ever roamed Noelle, and she had never, even for a moment, been cruel to Andie. Andie had grown up hearing one thing about the dragonborn, but her personal experience had been very different. And Andie certainly didn't feel evil herself. She needed to know more.

She slowed to a walk as she neared the giant doors of Leabherlann. At five steps, she glanced around her, making sure no one saw her coming. At four steps, she emitted a magenta wave of magic, concealing herself from sight. At three steps, she cast a charm to eradicate all sound—her breathing, footfalls, even her ponytail swinging against her back. At two steps, she sped up her central nervous system so that if she did find a book, she'd be able to read and comprehend it in a matter of moments. At the final step, she cast one last incantation.

"*Spiorad.*"

She passed straight through the wood of the door like a soundless ghost. Inside, she moved like nothing, like time itself, through and around the few students trying to get in their last-minute studying. Soundless, swift, and unseen. She moved straight for the archives, that old enemy that refused to share its secrets-if it even had any-hope that tonight of all nights would be different. As she approached the entrance, she found herself in the exact spot where she'd heard the voices before.

The feel of the place was different, thicker. There was something magical about the space now and it made Andie uneasy. She lifted her hand and let it rest in the air for several moments, just feeling the energy and the weight of the atmosphere. Then her eyes snapped open. Security spells. Her first instinct was to wonder if after all this time, someone had finally started paying attention, finally started noticing the goings-on of the dank and dusty archives.

She could try to enter anyway; after all, she recognized that she was an incredibly powerful sorceress. She'd excelled in her studies so far and she'd been studying spells for years. Her only problem had been control. However, she decided against it because if she tried to enter and overestimated her ability, there would be no going back. Her life and her father's would be over in an instant.

One good thing came out of that now barred entrance. Andie knew, without a doubt, that there was something important in the archives. Something worth hiding. Something maybe even worth killing for. She couldn't be sure if those precautions had been taken against her specifically, but she knew that there was something back there and that, come sorrow or destruction, she would find it.

She journeyed up and over to the restricted section

of the main area of Leabherlann, flipping through the old books just as something to do. Book after book after book, just as she had done a hundred times or more over the last few months. And, of course, she found nothing. Absolutely nothing. She threw the book into a corner and held her head, uncertain if she would explode from the sheer weight of her frustration. But then an idea came to her, one she should have had months ago.

She whipped around to make sure she was alone. Once certain of that, she closed her eyes and opened her palms toward the ceiling; she released herself, her magic, the dragon essence inside of her and it seeped out into Leabherlann like a million waves of violet light. The magic passed through shelves, slipped between books, moved to levels above and below her. She hadn't meant for it to go so far, but only a dragonborn would have been able to see it anyway. And it felt good. Unbelievably good. It wasn't often that she had an opportunity to release that side of herself, to truly give in to everything that she was and, even then, she wasn't realizing the full potential of her might.

Still, the magic felt like life surging in her bones and power running through her blood. Soon, the seepage began to pool in a corner not far from where she was standing. She turned to follow it, her eyes still closed, simply moving her feet to the direction from which the magic called. When she reached the corner, she opened her eyes.

The magic had worked flawlessly. In her Soul Matter and Para-Corporeal Explorations class, they'd covered variants of astral projection stemming from the earliest Cycles of the new Age. Needless to say, Andie had excelled in that section of study. She'd sent out part of her spirit to search for books on her kind, the dragonborn, and it had worked.

She stood there—half relishing long-awaited success and half cursing herself for not thinking of it sooner—looking down on a small heap of aged and dusty books. They looked practically discarded and had been thrown there quite some time ago, with no apparent concern for how they landed. She grabbed all of them and placed them in her bag; she didn't even check their titles, as her instinct told her they'd be of some use. Her magic may have been beyond her control, but it was never wrong.

She made it back to the main level of the Leabherlann and found the most secluded table in sight. She laid the books out in front of her. Seven dusty and average looking volumes, probably as old as Leabherlann itself. She began flipping through the pages hungrily, madly, her increased central nervous response allowing her to consume the words on the page at a superhuman rate. But it wasn't just reading that she could do better; the spell had improved all her senses and just then she heard him. Tarven. Judging from the sound, she figured he was just entering the library, whispering excitedly with someone, roughly three hundred yards from where she was sitting. She stopped reading and started listening.

"What are we supposed to do now?" Tarven asked.

"There is no 'we,' not yet. Not until you've proven yourself."

"What have you asked me to do that I haven't done? I've been to hell and back for you people and still you all treat me like some kind of child or outsider."

"I'm sorry, are those labels not applicable to you?"

"I understand that there's a plan in place and I even understand how small my role in it is. All I'm asking is for the potential to grow in the organization. Give me a chance to give you the proof you need. I won't fail you."

"It would seem you already have. Do you understand what's happening? Do you have any idea how close certain people are to our secrets? You've taken your eye from the target and it's nearly cost us the fruition of a plan that's been in play since before you were born, boy. At this very moment, amendments are being made because you left this organization open to assault. And you think you've earned a place at the table? You want to be involved in the conversations of big, scary men when you can't even clean your own mess. Hear me now, Tarven Stirmliir, you have failed on such a monumental scale that it's a wonder I haven't been ordered to permanently remove you from the equation. But be certain of this: should you continue to fail, should you fall short of our expectations, we will rain down a wrath upon you that will burn even your ancestors in their graves. You now walk the thinnest of lines and, speaking for the entire organization, I sincerely hope you fall. I savor the thought of your demise."

Andie heard them stop moving. Even at over a hundred yards, she could hear Tarven's heartbeat increasing. She could hear his skin tightening as he made fists of his hands. She grew tense. What was Tarven involved in? Who was the other voice? What kind of trouble was Tarven in? How great was the danger? Would she lose him? Could she help him? Whoever Tarven was with started walking again. Tarven waited a moment and then he started walking, too.

"As it is," the mysterious man continued, "You're uniquely placed to solve the problem you've allowed to develop. This will be your last chance. Will you rise to the occasion or will you fall too deep to recover?"

"We won't need to have this conversation again," Tarven said.

"That's not what I asked you."

"Yes. I'll rise."

Andie grabbed the books and then hid under the table. She cursed herself for waiting so long; even though most of the lights had been turned off already, she shouldn't have waited so long to conceal herself. It was stupid and arrogant, and she'd very nearly been caught. She continued listening as Tarven and the mysterious figure passed where she'd been sitting. The way she was hiding under the table prevented her from getting a look at the man's face, but his voice sounded familiar. Maybe. The two of them continued forward without a word and then went down to the archives. Andie stopped being able to hear them and she guessed it was due to whatever magical charms had been placed on the entrance to protect it.

She spread her books out on the table again, now worried about Tarven and the people he seemed to be in bed with. And for the first time since she'd taken off running, she thought back on Raesh in the ruins. It had not been a truly successful day. Yet, all she could do at that point was try to read through the material she'd found for the truth about her ancestry.

She made it pretty far before the day caught up with her and she was unable to keep her eyes open or her head up.

CHAPTER EIGHTEEN

THE SPELL HAS ALREADY BEEN CAST AND AS SHE STANDS there, high upon the mountain top with her people covering the cliffs and precipices around her, she knows there is no turning back. She and her people are standing still, stoic against the wind and the beating wings of their impending doom. She does not know how high they are; too high to see the ground and yet surely it must be somewhere below them. Grass. Land. Safety. Up here on the mountain they have no space to run, no place to hide, no safety or shelter to hope for. All they can do is wait for the purple storm of the incantation to wash over them, kill them where they stand.

They can see it in the distance—purple, as wide as the horizon and as tall as the space between earth and sky. The spell. They don't know who cast it, or maybe they do and it just doesn't matter because they know that there is nothing in their power they can do to stop it. On and on it rolls, closer by the second, as loud as the cries of a million dying souls. It is like fire and ice and wind and silence and roar and death and beauty and all the seasons of the year. It is stunning, in its own deadly way. They are all there, on that impossibly large mountain, staring at the thing they know is coming to kill them.

Silently, yet collectively, they wonder who could be so powerful. Who could have the might and the sheer hatred to cast such a spell? Such an irreversible and destructive spell? There are many millions of them there upon the mountain, gazing out across the vast expanse of nothing before them as the violet storm of the future rolls in to raze them. As it nears them, it begins to change color and where the space between the earth and sky had once been purple, it is now a dark, ominous gray. It is a gray that must've come straight from the grave, straight from all the worst of failure and suffering. Nobody will say it. Nobody will even dare to think it. But they all know, they all feel it somewhere within themselves and somewhere in the spaces between them. If the spell reaches them, their entire race will be wiped out.

The people—every soul upon the mountain—begin to panic. Before, there was silence, a kind of peace about them as if they had some time in the past decided on grace in defeat. But now, they are louder than the storm of the spell itself, screaming, crying, wanting to *flee or even dive off the mountainside. They know they're all going to die.*

Saeryn, who is the only one to have remained quiet amidst the pandemonium, looks at the storm in full, not flinching or even blinking. She has decided. If this is her last day, her final hour, she will not spend it in tears. She will not give over to fear or break herself with suffering. There is no fate that could find her that could steal her poise, her strength. "It is only death" she thinks to herself.

She takes a deep breath and prepares to make a final effort to save her people. She will try to call for help. She stretches out her arms to both sides of herself, reaching for the magic, all of it, all the power and spirit of her doomed race. She knows that if she can pull enough magic to herself, she can send a distress signal of sorts, though it is hard work with her people so afraid, so disoriented. Their magic is fueled in part by their emotion, which makes it stronger, but it is also fueled by their concentration, and that seems to be a difficult task for them right now. And who could be calm watching their own death approach?

She senses her bones and her blood filling with magic, brimming with the ability of her entire race. She lifts her head and opens her mouth, allowing a light brighter than anything on earth to fly up and out into the sky and beyond. A plea for mercy, aid, and protection. If no one answers...

"Help!" she screams, releasing the sound as a further emission of light racing toward the cosmos.

"Perhaps it is too late" she thinks as she looks out across her people, terrified and screaming themselves hoarse. She quiets her spirit, calms her mind. "I will not lose my peace today" she thinks, "Even if I lose my life." There is something strong about her then, some new and brilliant felicity charging through her bones. The behemoth spell looms nearer.

"If there is a single willing force in all creation, help us now."

ANDIE WOKE to find a hand on her shoulder. Someone had shaken her awake. The first thing she saw was the library floor, much closer than it should have been. She must've fallen asleep and slipped from her chair. She wondered why the fall didn't wake her. She'd known she was tired, but not enough to fall asleep and knock her head on the floor without even stirring. Just as she was thinking of falling, her head and hip began to ache. She touched her throbbing temple but the hand came away without blood. Her hip felt like it had a bent nail in it. She rubbed her head and tried to regain her sense of self, her presence of mind. It wasn't until she tried to calm herself that she noticed she was panting and terrified. The dream she'd had was half remembered; it was like her mind had been invaded by a heavy and unrelenting fog.

"Bad dream?"

Andie turned her eyes up. The hand belonged to Yara, who was smiling down at Andie in the way people smile when they want to comfort someone. Behind Yara was Professor Harrock and a group of students and staff all staring down at her. She hadn't even realized that many people were still in the library. So many eyes looking at her, wondering about her condition and probably her sanity.

"Why are all these people here?" Andie asked Yara, trying her best not to sound rude.

"I don't think they really had a choice," Yara said, looking at Andie even harder. "We all came running when we heard you."

"What? What are you talking about?"

"You called for help, Andie. You screamed for it. I heard you seventeen floors up. It made my blood run cold the way you screamed. It's like you thought you were dying. Was it just a dream? Do you need help?"

Andie was confused. How could she have been screaming? And now she saw the true expression on every face: they thought she was some kind of helpless thing, some child who had no other recourse to action than to scream for help. They gawked at her like some kind of specimen in a jar.

"I'm sorry. I don't know what happened," Andie

said, shaking her head as if to illustrate her bafflement. "I don't remember any dream."

"But you're not hurt?" Yara asked.

"No. No, I don't think so."

"Well, in that case," Yara said, her expression suddenly turning amused, "I think we can send all the would-be heroes away. Alright everyone, calamity evaded. Go home, go back, go away."

The crowd dispersed, though not without some parting glances at Andie. Yara turned back and reached her hands out to Andie. She helped pull her to her feet and then hugged her.

"Sorry," she said. "You just looked like you needed it. But if nothing else, you've given me one heck of an anecdote for the holidays."

"Thanks for getting rid of everyone. I hope I didn't scare you too bad."

"No worries. It's good for me to practice my heart attacks and nervous breakdowns. That way they won't take me by surprise in thirty years."

Andie was laughing before she could stop herself. Yara was always good for that. She realized her books were scattered all over the floor and she and Yara bent down to pick them up. It was a moment before she remembered that she was reading restricted books; perhaps Yara could be trusted, but some of the spectators had yet to leave and some had even come back for a last hopeful look. She gathered the books as quickly as possible.

Thankfully, Yara didn't seem to have paid attention. However, the librarian hadn't left yet and she was peering down at Andie's bag incredibly hard as if she knew something or had intentions of finding out. Murakami had made it back to work. Andie met her eyes and tried to stare her down, but Murakami wasn't so easily fought off and it was Andie who looked away first.

"Andie, your arm!" Yara said, her expression one of total shock.

Andie looked down to find the hairs on her arm had changed color to a light purple. Even her veins under her skin, though difficult to see, had returned to their natural purple state. Andie quickly jerked her sleeves down to cover the evidence and could only pray that her eyes and hair hadn't changed, too. There'd be no explanation for that. Yara continued to stare at her as if she'd never seen her before and Andie continued to stare back in utter fear. Could Yara be trusted? After all, didn't everyone hate the dragonborn? Andie looked around at the bystanders still hanging around. None of them had Yara's expression, but that didn't mean they hadn't seen. For all Andie knew, they were staring at her purple hair and byzantium eyes at that very moment.

"You, girl," Murakami said, slowly and with a dense suspicion in her voice. "You need medical attention."

"No. No, no, I'm fine."

"I see you, girl," Murakami said, advancing. "Something is not right. You are... not as you should be. You need to see someone."

"I- I- I'm fine."

"Medical attention, girl."

Without waiting to finish the exchange, Andie turned to run. It was all she could think to do.

CHAPTER NINETEEN

ANDIE FELT AS IF SHE WERE LOSING HER MIND. SHE'D somehow made it out of the University and had run all the way off campus before her legs gave out. Fortunately, there was no one else at the train station, only a few staff members. She could hardly breathe, and it wasn't just from the desperate sprint she'd made without stopping. It was the fear.

The world around her was an undulating blur, the buildings and signs and trees melting into a giant, unsteady mirage driven by her pounding heart. Her mind was hardly a mind at all, torn in too many directions and trying to regain control over a body that clearly couldn't resist the panic welling inside. Her eyes were either swimming or darting back and forth, trying to focus on something, anything. Her hands were trembling as if they'd been set to vibrate and her stomach was doing something very odd.

She felt not merely empty, but as if something had been drained from her chest, her blood, her very spirit. The fear was overwhelming, blinding. She'd been afraid before; in the nineteen years of her life she'd been scared many times, but only once before had she ever been scared like this. The night her mother was taken.

That was the last time Andie had to truly fear what she was, who she was by blood. The night the Searchers came and took her mother, Andie was terrified that they would take her, too, because she was a dragonborn. Dragon magic flowed in her veins. She was an outcast, a pariah, unwanted. That was the last time the world had ever come close to discovering the truth. And she would not have been able to deny it; how could she run from her own ancestry, her genetics?

Being in Leabherlann—not knowing how much of her magic had failed or for how long, with so many eyes watching her, and the look on Yara's face—was like being six years old again, kneeling in the grass while her house burned and her mother was taken from her. The world was peeking behind the curtain again, searching for her.

On top of that, she'd had a momentous afternoon. Learning Raesh had magic, learning he had so many other secrets, learning the true extent of the slaughter, the confirmation of the University's iniquity, Tarven's life-threatening danger, finally finding books, the poorly remembered dream that somehow still managed to haunt her, her magic failing. It had simply been too much.

When SKY 6 finally arrived, she shakily climbed aboard. Something about the staged gravity calmed her stomach, but not her mind. She'd never seen Yara look like that before, not even when she first woke up screaming on the floor. Or had she? Her mind was so clouded, so baffled by circumstance that she was beginning to forget what she remembered. Maybe Yara hadn't been looking at her at all or maybe it wasn't Andie's hair she'd seen. But what could it have been? Murakami didn't seem phased, but the words that came out of her mouth had shaken Andie to her core. What had happened? Had anybody seen what she was reading? What had she been screaming while she dreamed? What did she dream?

As her eyes struggled, she turned to gaze out of the window. She finally began to focus on the sight of the mountain, enormous and jagged, sliding away into the night as the train slithered down its side. She'd never realized what incredible speed the train had. If she listened closely, she could hear the low whistle of the wind being cut. The view calmed her some. Some of the weight was lifted from her shoulders as she watched the city of Arvall rise toward her with all its lights and glass monsters. From a perpendicular angle the city looked like a beautiful, convoluted starry night, planets and galaxy crashing together in a tumult of light, innovation, and time.

When the train reached the city, Andie thought of taking a cab home, but decided to walk. She was flustered and scared, and she needed to clear her head. She'd calmed some on the train, but she'd been so full of emotion that settling down merely a little wasn't enough. At last she decided that if someone had seen her true appearance and reported it, she'd just have to deal with it. There was nothing she could do about it now. Instead, she turned her attention to the dream. She seemed to remember a high point. A cliff, maybe. And a large cloud or mist. There seemed to be a woman. A woman with a mission. Andie worked hard to put the pieces together because she was starting to suspect that her dreams were something more. She wanted to figure out what they meant and what puzzle they fit together to make.

Nearing the apartment, she suddenly realized that she might not have the chance to be alone if she went inside. Raesh had no doubt told Carmen all about the day and of course Marvo would want to sit and chat. Andie just didn't have the stomach for company just then. Even more, for all she knew Yara had called Carmen about the episode in the library and everyone inside was waiting to comfort Andie the moment she came home. Raesh would be waiting.

Not ready to see anyone she knew, especially those

who cared about her, she ducked into a tavern on the way home, hoping for privacy and a place to read. She'd passed the place every day on her way home from the Academy and it seemed perpetually empty or scarce— perfect for her needs. It looked rather ominous at first glance. No windows, black paint, crossed axes on a thick, heavy door.

The tavern was dimly lit and sunken into the lower level of what seemed a fairly old building. The outside was painted with salt paint and it was hard to tell what it was made of, but from the inside she could see it was stone. She was confident no one would find her there, in a small, bleak tavern located in the narrowest bend of a winding road. On the rare occasions she was out with friends, they always stopped at bright and open bars with nice views and dance floors. No one would be looking for her there.

She walked in, careful to avoid what looked like an unnaturally large glob of spit, and was met with the smell of grindleward—a nasty and addictive herb that was bought and sold on the black market. Grindleward usually meant you were probably among the worst possible crowd. There were also Glycerinnds, mountain pirates that also indicated horrible company.

"'Ave a drink teeny lass, if 'at be what you're a wantin'."

Andie turned to face the voice and found that she was being spoken to from behind the bar. The man could only be described as a wrinkled sack, with eyes as blue and as sad as Gordric's Pain, the famous fjord.

"Yes. Thank you," she said.

Before she could say what she wanted, the barman pulled down a glass the size of her head and filled it with beer as red as blood. She hesitantly accepted and then moved to an empty table near the fire. She pulled out her books, sipped her ridiculously large beer, which turned out to be delicious, and set to work reading again. All the spells she'd cast had worn off while she was sleeping, but now she had time to read at her own pace.

Not long after she'd settled in, the barman came over with a plate of food. It looked as if it could feed her entire Extinct Beasts of the Northern Lands class.

"Ask me, ye look right close to faintin' or tearin' asunder. I'll 've no expirin' of such a base thang as 'unger in this 'ere tav'rn."

"I'm actually... Thank you very much," she said, deciding against a further lecture.

But he wasn't listening. His eyes were going over the books she had so carelessly spread over the table. Her hands leapt up, but she put them back in her lap; it was too late to cover them then.

"Curious about the dragonborn, are ye?"

"It's... It's just research. For school."

"Then why be ye sweatin' 'n shakin' like a demon's got ahold of ye?"

She stared at him, totally lost as to what to say. Finally, he nodded and began to move away. Then he turned back.

"Ye best take care who sees ye wi' those," he said, his warmth replaced by a chilling gravity. "It ain't never been safe to look into such things. 'specially not in the last thousand years. This 'ere is a city what sees everythin'. Ye can't be so naïve as to think ye can get away wi' it."

He turned and left, but what he'd said had given her pause. Of course, he was right and she was being stupid. She'd never even been in this place before, had no idea who might frequent the establishment. But who was the barman? What did he know of the dragonborn? What she'd learned from the books so far was harrowing. It turned out that the seven books were journals; she'd only made it through three so far, but they were the journals of the families of the seven men and women who began Arvall's birth and commissioned the University. They told of the hatred and bloodlust the families held for the dragons and for the dragonborn. There were very few dragons left in Noelle by their time, but they hated them unrelentingly. The journals told the tale of how the families set about spreading that hatred across Noelle and once they succeeded, they assembled an army of sorcerers and sorceresses that numbered in the hundreds of thousands; all across Noelle the dragons were hunted and slaughtered, their vital organs sold for crates of gold and other various parts of their bodies preserved for use in powerful spells. From its earliest beginnings, the University had been a poisonous institution.

As the final dragons were murdered senselessly, the seven leading families of the newly established Arvall city used their influence to turn the evil against the dragonborn. They feared retaliation for the slaughter of the dragons, which the dragonborn had fought to protect, and they also feared that the blood of the dragonborn might hold the secrets to bringing the dragons back. The second slaughter was even worse than the first. It took at least a hundred strong sorcerers to kill a dragon, but only one stealthy man to kill a dragonborn. They were decimated in every way imaginable. The journals told of the streets literally running with blood. And with every death, the University grew in power and stature, its black marble hiding horrors galore.

Andie continued reading the journals, feeling sick more often than not. The barman visited her often, asking if she wanted more food, more beer, or more logs in the fire. He was kind, but she wasn't in the mood for company. Then he came and stood for a moment until she was forced to look up at him.

"Ye be in the University, and by the looks of ye, first year at the 'cademy. Tell me, ole Harrock still strutin' about wi' his theories of magic across time?"

Andie's face expressed her shock. He chuckled.

"Don't look so worried, dearie. I taught 'ere once. In another lifetime. They still holdin' 'at wretched winter ball?"

She couldn't help herself. She laughed.

"It *is* a pretty ridiculous tradition. All that dancing and formality," she said, trying to quiet the voice inside of her still wondering if Tarven was going to ask her.

In the hours that followed, Andie read avariciously, asking the barman questions whenever something didn't make sense. He formally introduced himself as Lymir. He was extremely knowledgeable about the dragonborn, about history in general, but he was always careful to speak softly, even after all the guests had left. It was nearly midnight when she finally came across what she was looking for. She turned the page of the fourth journal and gasped.

It showed an ancient portal, somewhere deep in the recesses of the University.

CHAPTER TWENTY

For a moment, she was breathless. For months, she had been searching for information on perhaps a hundred different things and of the few subjects she actually thought she had a chance of locating, the portal was nowhere near the top. This was a hope beyond hope. Instinctively, her head leapt up and she looked around her, lest someone should be looking over her shoulder or peering over from the counter. The bar was totally empty and Lymir had gone in the back to do whatever closing tasks he needed done. She was alone. She gazed back down into the pages in front of her, still not fully believing she'd found it. She felt like smiling, but not much of her body was moving at the time.

"What a day," she managed out loud.

Her search for the portal had been a complicated one; originally, it wasn't even part of her mission.

Roughly a month before, she'd still been wholly obsessed with all things dragon—including the dragonborn, dragon magic, the great slaughter, the spread of anti-dragon sentiment across Noelle, and even Amanna Deireadh, the mythical end of days event when the remnants of the dragonborn discovered the means to restore the dragons and wreak hellish revenge.

She'd tried everything: sneaking into restricted sections, asking professors, attempting to get into the archives, and even antique bookstores, which is where her father found *From Dragons to Men*. She'd had absolutely no luck and that was including the use of virtually every ounce of her considerable magical prowess. Then one day, during her failed research she remembered something. It was some legend she faintly recalled from childhood: a portal. Since then she'd been trying to find information on that as well, but she could barely even remember the legend.

When she finally returned to the present and her seat in the bar, it seemed several minutes had passed, but she couldn't be sure. She turned back to the page and began reading. The journal described a series of portals, most lost to history, that magically connected realms through time. The founding families had used the one portal they could find and control. It was how they'd acquired so much knowledge when they'd been cut off from the rest of civilization for all those years.

The writer of the journal, Jacobi of House Clio,

wrote of how they'd studied the entire history of Shaeyara from its birth. They'd gone back as far as three Life Ages of the Earth and seen a world of pure darkness and void, a time when life was fleeting and hard and perilous. It mentioned that they'd made one—and only one—voyage to the future, but it did not say what they saw there, only that it affected them greatly and caused them to vow to never look forward again.

Jacobi wrote that the portal eventually proved dangerous when some members found they could use the portal as more than simply a looking glass. Their better senses prevailed and the unanimous decision was the portal should be magically sealed and remain so for all time. Apparently, many battles had been fought in a bloody war for the power of the portal; that war soon destroyed the portal.

At the bottom of the page, several blank lines after Jacobi finishes telling of the war, she wrote a single statement.

It is believed by all that the portal of Scáthán Ama was destroyed in that great and wasteful war of avarice, and perhaps it is so—but I believe this doorway may still exist.

As if he knew she was thinking about him, Lymir emerged from the back of the room and traveled around the bar, coming out to stand just near the table. He was still wiping one of his giant beer glasses and smiling like he was rather self-satisfied. She held up Jacobi's drawing of the portal.

"Lymir, do you know anything about this portal? Have you ever heard of it before?"

"'At be the portal of Scáthán Ama," he said, the color draining from his face. "A most wicked thing 'at is. All the legends be of grand times 'n gold 'n terrific adventures through history 'n space, but 'at ain't the whole story. Not by a half."

Lymir looked genuinely perturbed. Andie almost regretted asking as she watched the drawing's effect on Lymir. He obviously knew something, had maybe even experienced something. She had a moment of hesitation, but she had to know.

"Lymir, please," she said.

"When I be much younger, younger than you now, girl, I was a student at the University. In them days we knew what was underneath the mountain. They even let students go down to look at it. We'd write out our lessons in the shadow of the thing. Wasn't supposed to be no hanging 'round under it, but there was never anyone 'round to enforce 'at rule. We'd spend whole afternoons down 'ere wi' it. Then one day, three of the boys what was down 'ere wi' us decided to go up to touch it. Understand, 'at was somethin' we never dared afore. Soon as they laid their fingers on it, the bloody thing lit up like a star breakin' free and took the three boys. 'N it sucked all the air from the room, too. What of us was left almost suffocated to death.

"It turned out 'at it had happened afore. The bloody University had covered it up. Didn't want anyone deciding to skip this school because 'ere was a deadly... thing in the basement. A bunch of boys and girls had been sucked up over the years. Magic seal or no, the blasted thing couldn't be touched. Of course, the parents put up such a fuss 'at the University 'ad to either close down or put the thing somewhere else."

"I see they're still open," Andie said.

"And how."

For a moment, he simply stared down at the drawing, clearly reliving the sight of seeing those boys sucked up.

"Aye, it was sealed up. But don't believe everything you read. I don't trust them at that school. You seem like a curious girl, dearie," he said, looking down at Andie as if she were some fragile thing he'd been charged to protect. "You be careful not to mettle. People 'ave been hurt for far less things than what you're lookin' into. Don't pry."

He said the last part with a point and wave of his finger that was so emphatic she inadvertently promised out loud. Though from the look on his face, they both knew she couldn't be expected to keep her word.

After Lymir had returned to cleaning up, casting the occasional glare of suspicion, Andie read a little while longer and managed to finish her cranium-sized beer. Her dragon blood gave her a naturally high tolerance level, but that didn't stop her eyes from beginning to roll in their sockets.

She stared into the fire, trying to focus. She began to remember bits and pieces of her dream, possibly from the alcohol. There was screaming. And the woman at the precipice was calling for help. She thought she could feel her magic growing stronger in her veins, which she quickly chalked up to the gargantuan beer. It suddenly occurred to her that the portal might have something to do with her dreams. It didn't make sense, of course, but she couldn't shake the feeling. It might have something to do with the room in the back of the archives, too. Her dreams had intensified ever since she heard the voices through the door.

Then she just knew. It was the portal that was behind the door.

Some minutes after her epiphany, Andie was finally ready to go home. She began packing up the journals and picking over the plate Lymir had brought her, as there was still over half of the enormous helping left. Just as she was slinging her bag over her shoulder and getting ready to say goodbye to Lymir, the door opened. It was Tarven. It was hard to tell who was more surprised to see him: her or Lymir.

"What are you doing here?" she asked, trying not to

think of the conversation she'd overheard in Leabherlann.

"I saw you come in and I just wanted to know if it was okay if I joined you for a drink."

"Tarven, I've been in here for hours. Have you been standing outside this whole time?"

"Well, practically," he said.

She got the distinct impression he was lying, which bothered her. If he hadn't followed her, then how had he found her there? But he smiled that impossible smile of his and she was won over. He moved to sit down, but then he caught Lymir's eye. She had no way to describe the look they shared, it seemed one of ominous recognition.

"Why don't we grab a drink somewhere else?"

Andie looked over at Lymir, who pretended not to notice and kept wiping glasses.

"Okay. Sure," Andie said, suspicious in spite of herself.

On the way out, she looked back at Lymir and that time he was ready for her. He moved one of his worn fingers slowly to his mouth, a silent plea for Andie to keep her secrets to herself.

CHAPTER TWENTY-ONE

As they were leaving the tavern, Andie was considering Tarven. Not only was he caught up in something that sounded beyond dangerous, he was clearly not very good at whatever his job was supposed to be carrying out. His position, his very existence, was on the line. Then of course there was the business with Raesh and whatever Tarven or his friends, or Tarven *and* his friends, had done to frighten him so deeply to his core.

These things in connection with the many things Tarven knew that he wasn't supposed to know was beginning to wear on Andie, and not merely wear on her, but wear her down. How could she trust him knowing everything she knew? He'd had a full day with her and hadn't even known it.

"You know, it's later than I thought," she said. "A lot later. I'm actually pretty tired."

To give authenticity to the charade, Andie looked at her phone to check the time. Her eyes bulged. It was almost four in the morning. As if they were merely waiting for an acknowledgement of the time and their limit, her eyes got so heavy she bent her head.

"Oh," Tarven said, clearly searching for something persuasive to say. "You... come on, you're in the Academy now. Live a little."

"How original," she responded.

She was as unimpressed as she sounded, though she meant to sound more joking. She tried to make up for it.

"I mean, what are we going to do at this time of the night anyway? And, just out of curiosity, how did you find me?"

"I told you, I saw you go into that tavern."

"No, you didn't."

Tarven stopped in his tracks. He stood there, looking at the ground, and breathing irregularly. She'd caught him lying again and he knew it.

"There's no way you followed me from the University," Andie continued. "So, unless you just happened to be in the neighborhood and happened to walk into that tavern and happened to see me and decided to lie, you must've had some device or something that helped you find me. So, how did you do it?"

She'd decided to get the truth out of him and was doing it before she'd even really thought about. She hoped going on instinct could work twice in one day, but she was also conscious of the two-way street of suspicion. The last thing she needed was to arouse his suspicion by over-saturating him with her own, especially considering the mystery and danger surrounding whoever it was he was working for. That fear grew in her mind as she waited for Tarven to respond.

Finally, he said, almost sheepishly, "Let me walk you home."

Torn amongst fear, uncertainty, suspicion, and the growing desire for self-preservation born out of the ubiquitous cautions to mind her business, Andie caved. "Coward," she thought to herself.

They walked on, quietly at first, but then they began to chat about trivial things. Somewhere between Avenue 664 and Maith Root, Tarven showed surprising dexterity and slipped his hand in hers almost without her knowing. Contrary to her better judgement, she allowed herself to forget about the secrets surrounding him— well, not forget, exactly.

There was no way she could forget the cloud of deceit Tarven moved in, but she couldn't help how much she liked him. There were times, like that very moment, when he was near perfect. Sweet, charming, handsome, and all-consuming. She definitely had mixed feelings, but she was aware now of something much stronger than that beneath. She didn't know if he had a way with women or a way with her, but it was a fantastic way. Sometimes it seemed surreal that he should be giving her so much attention, that he should be so interested in her. He could have anyone in the entire school—she was pretty sure he was aware of this —and maybe even all of Arvall.

"So, what happened to you in the library?" he asked. "That was some screaming fit."

She had to think for a moment. She couldn't say that she'd seen him in Leabherlann, as she had hid when he passed her. But she also knew that he was supposed to have work that time of the evening. He should have been in a completely different wing of the University. Or maybe he'd been lying all along. Or maybe someone just called him with the news. Who knew?

"I just had a bad dream," she said. "A really, really bad dream. And on top of that, I've been feeling a little overworked lately. Just a bad combination."

"Want to talk about it?"

The honest concern in his voice only further warmed her to him.

"Not really. Maybe some other time. I think the best thing to do might be to drop a class to lighten the stress."

"But you were doing so well."

"Yeah, but it's been really tough. The Academy's been a lot harder than I expected. What about you? How's your hortological work in the gardens? All about understanding the life of the plant, right?"

"And I am struggling to understand and to not strangle the life from said plants."

She laughed and he smiled at her. That smile.

"Actually, I could use some more of your help out there."

"Funny you should ask. I'm actually eager to get back there and practice my magic. With you."

Half an hour and a tremendous amount of flirting later, they arrived at Marvo's restaurant. As if on Cue, Raesh appeared in the window and of all the things in the street for him to look at his eyes went straight to her and Tarven. Noting this, Andie tried to wrap things up with Tarven quickly.

"Okay, so I'll-"

Before she could finish, Tarven pulled her into a kiss. Her immediate instinct was to resist, for Raesh's sake, but, much to her own personal chagrin, she mildly swooned in his arms. Her hesitation and inhibitions swept away, she kissed him back with everything she had. She would try to describe it in words to herself later, but there were none. It was perfect.

"Come to the Winter Festival with me," he said.

The look in his eyes was the one Andie imagined in

the eyes of every man risking his pride for something, someone, he truly wants. He seemed so beyond genuine, as though he not just wanted her there, he needed her there.

"Yes. Of course, I'll go with you."

Simultaneously, she was convincing herself that she had been insane to doubt him. Certainly, there were things about him that didn't make sense to her, but how could she cast doubt on him just because she didn't understand? After all, she was the one who was blatantly lying to everyone, every day. Right then she decided that he was kind, trustworthy.

Tarven turned and left.

Raesh was still standing in the window. Slack-jawed. Devastated.

Somehow, he seemed like a child there; it was like he was lost or thought he was lost. Maybe he was frozen there, stuck in his disbelief, or even paused by his own volition until his mind and his heart caught up to each other. Andie couldn't face him and yet couldn't quite turn away, leaving herself turned half away from him, looking back at his hurt expression almost over her shoulder. Neither of them was moving, like some agreement of shame and despair. She kept thinking to herself "That didn't happen. That didn't happen. That didn't happen." Yet the taste and the feel of Tarven's lips were still on her mouth.

Unconsciously, her hand rose to her mouth and felt the skin there and it was almost like she was trying to confirm or deny it. Raesh still hadn't moved an inch and even when Marvo came up behind him, smiling and chattering away, he remained still as a statue. When Marvo found his son was unresponsive, he turned over his shoulder and called.

He still hadn't seen Andie in the street. As if the situation weren't bad enough, Carmen came hurrying over to check on her cousin. But she'd hardly made it to the window when she saw Andie outside, not ten yards from the glass. She simply pointed outside. Marvo turned his head and found Andie. His mouth threw questions at her, but she couldn't answer. She really couldn't. And then Carmen was anxiously pointing at something behind Andie.

The next thing Andie knew, she was on the ground. A car was speeding down Rholdan, its exhaust blowing vermillion as its crystals died from age and probably ill-keeping. Andie gazed around her and found no one. She realized she must have jumped aside by some survival instinct. When she looked back at the restaurant, she had just enough time to see Raesh storming away into the back, Carmen following close behind and obviously trying to get him to calm down. Marvo was hurrying out of the front of the store to come check on Andie, but she held her hand up to stop him.

"It's not right," she thought to herself. "He shouldn't have to come and check on me, not when his son needs him more. I can't believe that happened. I can't believe I let it. He'll never forgive me."

And of that last part she was almost certain. Raesh had a good heart, a pure heart, but everyone had their limits. And what would it mean for Carmen? Would she decide to take her cousin's side? Were there really sides? Was it coming to that? And if Carmen left, she was sure to take Yara and anybody else she'd introduced Andie to. Even Fohrn in the library. And Marvo. But she couldn't lose Marvo, too.

She picked herself up and walked right by Marvo, answering his multitude of questions with a curt guarantee of her wellbeing, never stopping her forward motion. And she never stopped moving until she reached her bed and then she collapsed into a breathing ball of shame and regret.

The moment was made even harder because she was so happy to have finally been invited to the festival by Tarven. So much joy and remorse, all at once. She thought of her dad, far away in Michaelson, who she knew was probably thinking of her, too. He would know what to say, and if he didn't he would hold her, kiss her cheek, and tell her something sweet beyond comprehension. She'd never wanted so much to be back home.

She waved her hand above her and cast a silence

charm, blocking out everything in the world. The day had been impossibly long and she just wanted it to be over. She wanted to skip ahead to a time when things were okay again. She closed her eyes and tried to rest. It was nearly five o'clock. She had to get up and get ready in two hours.

CHAPTER TWENTY-TWO

TWO WEEKS PASSED AND EVERY RELATIONSHIP IN Andie's life changed.

She hadn't spoken to Raesh since that night. She saw him constantly, of course, in the restaurant and around the building. She even saw him at most of her hangout spots because he was the one who had shown them to her in the first place. She continued to help Marvo out, but she did less and less and he stopped asking her to do some of the things she'd been doing for months.

Raesh seemed fundamentally different during those weeks; he still went out with his friends and still worked the same schedule at the restaurant, but even when he smiled there was something beneath it. Something was maybe sad and maybe furious, but something that was, without a doubt, not Raesh. Yet he wasn't cold toward her. He certainly didn't put himself in a position to talk to her and he avoided her as often as possible, but when circumstance dictated he needed to interact with her he was as civil as imaginable. And that hurt her even more.

Whatever Raesh had or hadn't told Marvo, nothing much seemed to have changed. Marvo did what he could to keep them working in different areas or different schedules—after all, he wasn't an idiot—but outside of that he didn't treat Andie any differently. He spoke to her more often, if anything, and gentler, as if he'd thought it over and decided that she needed him more than his own son. More likely, however, was that Marvo and Raesh had had at least some minor conversations about Raesh's feelings for Andie and Marvo had decided to play mediator. He was a good man.

Carmen was more difficult; since that night her signals had been all over the place and Andie couldn't quite pin down what Carmen wanted or expected, how she truly felt. Andie never knew what side of Carmen she was going to get: it might be the same, playful Carmen Andie had grown close to, or it might be the sullen Carmen who seemed to prefer brooding and judgmental looks, or it might be an outright frustrated and dismissive Carmen, or it might be any one of ten other Carmens who presented themselves without reason or pattern.

It was clear that she was Andie's friend and equally as clear that she was Raesh's cousin. Andie accepted that Carmen had been placed in an impossible predicament and simply took her moods as they came, doing her best to let Carmen know that she understood the stunning difficulty of it all.

Andie's circle outside of Raesh, Marvo, and Carmen was small, but everyone else that she knew seemed to have taken sides. It was either Andie or Raesh. Most people chose Raesh, understandably. But Andie got to keep Yara and most of the students she'd met at the Academy, so things weren't so bad.

It was the morning of the Winter Festival and Andie was in Victory among the twisting, draping, floating plants. She was helping Tarven with an experimental cross-pollination of fuil glas and anáil fuar; it was for the mirror room, for the festival. There was a total of twelve mirror rooms in the University, but for the one thousandth festival they were using the Grand Mirror Hall of Terpsichore, designed and named in honor of one of the seven founding families. The mirror rooms were made by ancient magic and their texture, dimensions, and design could be changed at will, like spellglass, but only by the board members. The mirror rooms could also appear as one thing to all or as an individual fantasy to each dance couple. There was nothing like the mirror rooms in all of Noelle. Andie and Tarven had been hard at work; after all, no one wanted to be the person responsible for ruining a thousand-year-old celebration.

Andie's magic had grown steadily stronger since she'd started at the Academy and a strange surge in power had come to her over the last two weeks. The dragonborn was most feared because their magic was so heavily influenced by their mood—a frightened dragonborn could struggle to take on one adversary, but a dragonborn filled with rage could stand against an army.

The University understood this and worked diligently to instill fear in the dragonborn before slaughtering them; just another reason why the massacre was so catastrophically horrible. But, Andie had been happy the last two weeks. Incredibly happy. Tarven seemed to have undergone a change. He was more open with her and he didn't always seem as if he were hiding something. They were growing closer every day.

"You know, you're showing a lot of promise out here," he said. "Maybe you could work at the University one day."

"Yeah. Yeah, that's actually exactly what I want to do," she teased. "Stare at roots all day and wonder if the stem will be half a centimeter longer in two weeks or three."

"Don't forget the joy of working with the Seile."

"Oh, how could I forget. Best part of my day."

They both laughed. Tarven knew Andie enjoyed working in the gardens as merely a hobby, but he teased her often. Seile was a classification for plants that could shoot poison or psychotropic saliva as projectile crystals. Once they hit their target, the crystals would sink under the skin and disperse. Strong or knowledgeable sorcerers could use magic to delay the effects until they received medical attention. Humans almost always died.

Andie had taken careful note of Tarven's change over the past fortnight. His whole demeanor had changed and now she felt comfortable with him. She could say that she trusted him with no qualms. It was as if he'd finally decided to put her first and transcend whatever other dark dealings he had. She was no fool, and she remembered everything that had happened, but who was she to judge when she had so many secrets of her own? And it was just that thinking that lead her to want to change herself. She was tired of lying and hiding, and if anyone was there for her to talk to and share with it was Tarven. She'd decided to tell him the truth. Still, true to her cautious nature, she wanted to start with something small, or as small as she could get with the life and death secrets she kept.

"Tarven," she said, cautiously, like a fish testing waters. "Have you ever heard of a portal?"

"Sure. You know, big, lots of light, bridges across time and space, totally nonexistent."

"No, I mean here, in the University. A portal that no one talks about."

Tarven stopped and turned to her. There was a moment.

"You mean the portal that no one talks about because there's no such thing as a portal in the University."

He broke into a smile and it was obvious that he'd been joking with her. She smirked, briefly. She couldn't tell if he was joking because he was covering or because he honestly didn't know. There was a chance he had no idea what she was talking about. He was so knowledgeable that Andie always assumed he knew everything, but he was a student himself, after all. Even with his mysterious connections there was no way he could know everything about everything. Still, Andie being Andie, she pushed anyway.

"No, Tarven. I'm talking about something real. I'm talking about the portal of Scáthán Ama."

Instantly, he stiffened. It was like some kind of coagulant had been poured in his veins. He tried to shrug it off, but she'd already seen it.

"It's a myth," he said, flat. "That thing no longer exists. It's been sealed for centuries and even before that it had been moved. No one knows where it is. And that's assuming it's real and the whole story isn't some hoax, which many experts say it is."

This went totally against everything Lymir had told Andie at the tavern. One of them wasn't telling the truth. The difference was that Lymir had absolutely no reason to lie to Andie. Tarven did.

"Tarven, I think you're lying," she said. "Actually, I'm pretty sure of it."

"What do you know, anyway?" he snapped. "Every time I turn around, you've got some new theory or question about things that don't even concern you! You have no idea how horrible it was when the portal was here. The fear. The disappearances. The least you could do is show some respect for the people who died getting sucked through that thing. What about the thousands and thousands who died in the wars? Do you have any sensitivity at all for those people? Their families? Their suffering? Can you even fathom the catastrophe?"

"I'm sorry," she said. "I won't ever bring it up again."

Tarven walked a small, frustrated circle. Breathing hard and holding his head. Andie regretted not showing more concern for all those who suffered at the hands of the portal.

"I understand if you don't want to go to the festival with me anymore," she said.

Tarven exhaled a long breath and then turned to her, took her in his arms and held her for a minute, silently forgiving her. Then he let her go and kissed her cheek. Then her lips. They returned to normal.

"Of course, I do," he said. "I wouldn't miss it for the world. I'm sorry I snapped, Andie. I've just always been... sympathetic to large groups of people suffering or dying when it's not their fault. That portal changed things for so many people. For all of Shaeyara. It just gets to me. But you didn't deserve that and there is no possible excuse."

"Even though you just tried to give me one?" she asked.

He looked at her and she broke into a smile. He smiled, too. She was happy.

"Well, as much fun as I'm having out here with you and the twenty-foot roses, I have to go to class," Andie said.

"So, I'll see you tonight?"

"You most certainly will. Have fun with your plants. And, seriously, the roses freak me out."

She kissed him once more and then turned to leave. Before she did, she noticed a small plant reaching toward Tarven. It was incredibly attractive and the whole thing was no bigger than the palm of her hand; it had a long, thin stem and only four petals in its bloom. The petals and bloom were the color of bronze, but the stem was as black as the night sky over an old field. Its petals were waving languidly, though there was no breeze, and it seemed to be trying extraordinarily hard to reach Tarven. Andie leaned toward it and discovered it was making tiny, barely audible sounds, almost like it was breathing.

"What's this one?" she asked, pointing. "It's so cute."

"That little guy is Decepticatus."

"It almost looks like it's trying to touch you. What does it do?"

"Believe it or not, I have no idea."

"Shocking," she said.

She waved again and walked away. She couldn't see it, but Tarven was watching her the whole time.

CHAPTER TWENTY-THREE

Not fooled at all by Tarven's failed cover-up—
and even less by his pathetic attempt to accuse her—
Andie skipped class to try to investigate the portal room.
She knew in her heart, beyond all doubt, that it was still
in the University. And she knew where it was.

She made her way to Leabherlann, though with
some difficulty. The entire University was alive with the
preparations for the event. The school was also hosting
some eleven thousand dignitaries, heads of state,
relevant celebrities, and scholars, all of whom were
being housed in a specially erected condominium placed
in the mountainside above the University. The halls
were bustling with people decorating or cleaning or
giving tours to foreigners and important people. She was
also seeing several strange creatures from the lands

beyond Abhainn. They'd traveled a long way. Andie had to push her way through dense crowds.

She reached Leabherlann and even there she had to search for a quiet, secluded corner. She opened her bag and retrieved the enhancement items she'd bought the week before—she'd found them in a peculiar antique shop that Lymir had recommended. She turned each of them over, trying to decide what she would need going in and what she could save until later. Finally, she decided to put everything back except the craiceann, a gossamer magical veil in the androgynous shape of a human face.

Andie checked her surroundings once more and then lifted the craiceann to her face. She held it there. The light fabric began to cling to her face, and not merely cling but attach itself. It sealed itself to her skin around the edge of her hairline and then quickly began stretching, flowing down her neck, back, and chest, always clinging tight. At first it was as cold as ice, but as it finished covering her entirely, it began to warm to her body temperature. She took out a compact and checked her reflection. The craiceann had altered her appearance completely; it had even changed the shape and height of her body. She didn't look anything like herself.

She felt more confident with it on; at least now if something happened and she weakened or was distracted, her appearance wouldn't betray her. She was still careful around Yara. Nothing between them had been the same since that night in the library. Yara had been treating her differently and Andie couldn't tell if it was because Yara had seen her true self or because she'd found her screaming. The craiceann would ensure that didn't happen with anyone else.

Andie packed up her things and walked back to the center of Leabherlann to head in the direction of the archives. She passed some people she knew and decided to test the device.

"Hi, there," she said.

They looked up at her, right in the face, and didn't recognize her.

"Hi," Sheila said. "Have we met before?"

Andie grinned and left, now one hundred percent sure she was safe. "I should have tried this years ago," she thought.

Suddenly, incredible pain stabbed in her hand. She very nearly screamed out loud. Before she could recover from the shock of the first stab, another came. This time it lingered for a bit and she went down on one knee. The pain kept coming intermittently and she looked at her hand, turning it over furiously to try to find what was causing the pain. It nearly made her cry.

Then she saw it. The faint red glow in the center of her palm. The icon. In all the months she'd had it, it had always been a dim, pretty golden glow. Never once had it shone red. The longer she watched it the brighter it became and the more intense the pain became. Whatever magic the craiceann was using on her body, it was interfering with the icon, which was growing hot in the flesh of her hand. Ducking into an unoccupied aisle, Andie held her arm at the wrist, squeezing as hard as she could in an effort to close off the pain—the sensation was starting to shoot down her arm.

Once she was alone again, safely away from the eyes that had begun to watch her whimper in pain, Andie began an incantation. She had to stop the pain and she also had to try to stop the reaction of the icon, which would definitely send signals to the University, if it hadn't already. She recited the incantation for the pain; it dulled considerably, but her hand continued burning. It was clearly not going away completely as long as the craiceann and icon were acting on her body at the same time.

She cast another spell, one she'd learned from one of the founding family journals. It was designed to interrupt the ability of magical artifacts to emit magic at all. She said it quickly, not sure if she remembered the words or if it was too late. Just as the thought crossed her mind, she heard the doors of Leabherlann bang open. She ran to the end of the aisle, breathlessly scared.

"Andie Rogers!" a woman called.

Andie was rooted to the spot, no more able to move than she was able to change the course of events that had led her here.

"Andie Rogers!" the woman called again.

Andie thought the woman sounded genuinely concerned, which perhaps meant that the signal hadn't told them what was happening, only that something wasn't right. As the woman moved around a group of onlookers, Andie could see that she was small, but focused. The woman moved in an almost unnaturally straight line, coming straight down the center of Leabherlann in Andie's direction. And still Andie was frozen, terrified, wondering what she was supposed to do and how she could have been so stupid, so arrogant as to think she could fool an institution that had hundreds of years' worth of hunting and those it wanted destroyed. The woman—who had three men with her—kept coming, her short stride quick and her footfalls surprisingly heavy on the black marble.

Andie was seemingly paused, half leaning out from behind the bookcase, just watching the woman bear down on her. Her entire history was playing itself behind her eyes. Tarven. Raesh. Marvo and Carmen. Arvall. Michaelson. Her father, who she hadn't called in far too long. She skipped going home to see him last week in order to be in the gardens with Tarven and there were no words to express how much she regretted that then, as the end of her world bore down on her. At last, after what seemed a thousand years and also a single second, the woman came to a stop in front of Andie. The look her eyes gave was one Andie would never forget.

"Excuse me," the woman said, in a voice that was as lyrical as it was authoritative, "Andie Rogers?"

Andie's mouth opened for speech, but no words would come. It was all over.

"Have you seen her?"

Andie simply stared. It was impossible.

"What?" Andie asked, totally confused.

"Have you seen Andie Rogers? Do you know her?"

Andie almost laughed out loud. The spell had worked, and the icon was no longer sending whatever magical signal it had sent out before. It had managed to send no more than her name and the fact that she was in Leabherlann. And the craiceann was doing its work as well; the woman was staring right in Andie's face and didn't know. Andie tried to bury the smirk.

"No ma'am, I don't know anyone by that name," she said, realizing her voice had also changed.

"Hm. Have you seen anyone in distress? Anyone who looked like they were hurt or needed help?"

"No. I'm sorry, I've just been looking for texts for my exams."

The woman nodded and moved on. Andie allowed

herself mere moments to celebrate before moving on. If the pain in her arm were to flare again, it might not be something she could stop up so quickly. She hurried along, keeping a good distance between herself and the searching woman, and turned off into the archives.

At the entrance to the hallway, she paused. The craiceann was supposed to alter her appearance and hide her magic from virtually all defenses—at least the simple ones the University was likely to be using in a library—but she was still nervous. However, she had to admit that the magical device had already saved her life once and she had no reason to doubt it now. She took a single step across the threshold and found herself safely in the hallway.

She raced along the way, dashing past the peculiar and enticing volumes of history and study as she headed for the back room. All she could think of was the portal and the secrets it held. The secrets it could reveal. She reached the end of the path and turned the corner to find the door, just as she remembered it, just as she had seen it all those months ago. Without warning her head was filled; she'd almost forgotten how the voices overwhelmed her, how they weighed on her spirit and tore at her mind.

She kept walking, but the closer she got, the louder and wilder the voices became. She kept putting one foot in front of the other until she couldn't anymore. She moved her leg forward, but collapsed in a heap under the barrage of screams. She held her head, desperate to hold the screams in or perhaps keep them out, but they were so loud, so many. The voices were crying out for help. They were suffering. The voices in her head were more painful than the icon had been, and even her hand was growing hot again. She didn't know what to do.

She crawled the remaining feet to the door and placed her hands on it. It was warm from the sheer volume of magic on the other side. She suddenly pulled her hands away, bewildered. Sorcerer's magic, though powerful, is cold. It must feel normal to those without dragon blood, but to a dragonborn only dragon magic is warm. The magic on the other side of the door is warm. She put her hands back on the door and held them there. Soon enough she felt it: the dragon magic igniting in her blood. It swam through her, burning in her chest and stomach. The dragon magic in her grew stronger and stronger, and if it wasn't for the craiceann, she probably would have reverted to her natural appearance. She needed to break into that room. Instinct moved her. She closed her eyes.

"Who are you?" she asked. "What do you want?"

There was no answer.

She reached up to try the handle, but was thrown several feet back by the defensive magic. She knew then, that to get into the room she would need help. Just then she heard someone coming. She panicked. It took all of her strength to regain her feet, but as soon as she did, she ran.

As her feet moved, her mind planned. She would find help. She would get into that room. Not only to stop the voices and the dreams, but also to save something. Maybe her own life.

CHAPTER TWENTY-FOUR

By that evening, Andie had discarded the craiceann and her icon had returned to its normal state. The searing pain vanished completely about an hour after Andie removed her disguise and she'd heard no more from the woman who was searching for her, though she knew she would have to face her sooner or later. She would need to remove the blocking spells Carmen had shown her; being searched for was suspicious enough.

She was at Carmen's apartment—Carmen lived in the Publishing District, twenty blocks away from Marvo's restaurant—getting ready for the first night of the festival. The first night is traditionally the night of dancing at the Founder's Ball, with the rest of the week, or month in this case, being designated for a plethora of other means of celebration. Yara was also there, strangely her old self. Andie assumed Yara had come to some decision within herself and as much as Andie wanted to know what it was, she decided not to press her luck.

Carmen was in a stellar mood and Andie was incredibly grateful that that side of Carmen was the one that manifested that night. Carmen was laughing, teasing, fantasizing as if there were nothing more between them. Andie had a burning desire to ask how Raesh was; she knew that the night would be a hard one for him. It was hard for her, too. She couldn't pretend that Raesh wasn't important to her, even if she couldn't care for him the way he cared for her. But she buried all of that at the base of her mind, reveling in having Carmen and Yara as her friends again.

"I need to congratulate you again on this dress," Yara said, holding Andie's dress against her own body and spinning to bring out the true luminousness of the dress. "I can't believe your sense of style is this good."

"It's not," Carmen interjected. "I picked that. Should've worn it myself."

"And I hate both of you," Andie said with a smile, snatching the dress from Yara.

Carmen had taken Andie to the store, took one look at her figure, and chosen her dress in under five minutes. The dress was ankle-length, the color of a bronze sun. It flattered Andie in every way a dress should and complemented her hair. She thought to herself that it would probably look good with her natural hair color and her byzantium eyes, too, but that wasn't an option. Not yet.

"Let me be the first to say it," Yara said.

"First to say what?" Andie asked.

"How lucky you are. I'm not going to go weak in the knees when I say this, but Tarven is gorgeous."

"I second that," Carmen said, beginning to apply her foundation.

"I don't want to cross any lines here, but that boy takes up half of my many, many fantasies. And of all the girls in the Academy, the University, and even Arvall, he chose you."

"You probably don't know this," Carmen began, "But most of the girls at the University are wishing they were you tonight. That or wishing they could rip your heart out, but either way is a pretty good omen, I'd say."

"I feel lucky," Andie said. "I almost feel like I'm in a dream. And if I am, I hope I won't wake up, not this week and hopefully not at all. I'm happy, really happy, for the first time in a long time and I have Tarven to thank for that. I nearly gave up waiting for him to ask."

"Trust me, the rest of us saw it coming," Yara said. "I may or may not have secretly tried to poison you, but, you know, bygones and all that."

The girls laughed and chatted excitedly about the night. Andie was anxious to see whether or not the attendees would like the cross-pollinated species she and Tarven had put up. Yara and Carmen were beside themselves about the full night of dancing.

"I'm surprised you two are so excited for this," Andie said. "I know it's the thousandth year, but haven't you been to this festival two or three times already?"

"Yes. And no," Yara said.

"We usually sneak off with our dates about a third of the way through," Carmen added. "It's really kind of stuffy with all the professors and faculty there. All these years and we've never actually danced at one of these things. We come, listen to the introductions and brief, mandatory history, drink the ale, watch the faculty members take the floor, and then we disappear into the night."

"Every time."

"What could be more interesting than the Winter Festival?" Andie asked, incredulous.

"Nothing," Yara said. "Absolutely nothing. Which is why we'll be staying this year."

"Probably," Carmen added with a sly smile.

Carmen and Yara continued talking, but Andie became silent. An idea had dawned in her mind and it only took a few short moments for her to begin to fixate on it. If all the professors, faculty, and students were celebrating in the mirror rooms and down in the city of Arvall itself, it would mean that Leabherlann would be empty. Totally empty. In fact, she'd already read the

211

announcement saying that the library would be closed that evening due to the celebration.

As she stood there with her bronze dress draped over her arms, she knew without a doubt that she might never have that kind of opportunity again. Of course, the spells would still be in place, but there would be no eyes around. She'd have an entire night of uninterrupted time to get into the archives, open the door, and discover what the portal could tell her about herself and the world. And she had two potential accomplices standing right in front of her.

"I want you two to help me break into a place," she said.

"Sure," Carmen said immediately. "And right after, we'll assassinate in Taline."

"And resurrect the dragons and bring on Amanna Deireadh," Yara added joyously.

They laughed, playfully shoving Andie and returning to getting dressed.

"I'm serious," Andie said, as solemn as the grave. "I want to break into somewhere inside the University that's been sealed shut with powerful magic. If we're suspected, we get expelled. If we're caught, we probably get worse. I've tried to do it myself half a dozen times, but I need help. Two powerful sorceresses who I trust more than anyone else in the world could help me do this. If they had a mind to."

Carmen and Yara stared at Andie for a long time.

When they were satisfied she was serious, they turned to each to share something only they understood—a sort of timid curiosity perhaps—and then looked away. A few tense moments passed while Andie stood waiting, her hands anxiously made into fists and her temples beginning to sweat. Had she made a mistake?

"I'm in," Carmen said, suddenly looking up from her feet. "If you need my help, of course I'm in. I'd do anything for you."

"Yeah. Count me in, too," Yara said. "You won't be off having illegal adventures without me. You're strong and brilliant, so whatever you're after must be critical. I'm there."

"Thank you," Andie said.

She wanted to say more, but couldn't. She was overwhelmed by her own gratitude. She looked up to see them smiling at her.

"What?" she asked.

"Nothing," Yara said, coyly. "It's just nice to see you break from the sweet, doe-eyed girl habit."

"Agreed," said Carmen, devilishly. "Mischievous looks good on you."

They all smiled and held hands. Andie knew then, beyond a shadow of a doubt, that no matter what differences of unvoiced things lay between them, these girls were her friends. Her best friends.

"I'm getting too excited," Carmen said. "Sneaking

around, getting past hooded monitors. It's more fun than I thought I'd be having tonight."

"We usually do this stuff pretty often to hook up with boys, or drink, or whatever else we decide to get into. But breaking into the University. Priceless."

"Well, I'm glad you're so eager," Andie said, beginning to enjoy herself now. "But I should warn you, it could be dangerous. There's already powerful magic in place and there's bound to be more of it since everyone will be out celebrating."

"Oh. Oh, well excuse me," Carmen said.

"Good heavens!" said Yara. "Danger? Like real danger?"

"Perhaps we've been too hasty accepting, darling."

"Yes, yes, quite so, how right you are."

"We should back out now, if at all possible. Wouldn't want to be implicated."

"Oh, no, no, no, no, no. That simply wouldn't do."

"Thank goodness we've come to our senses, Yara."

"Yes, Carmen, quite fortunate, indeed. We were very nearly made criminals."

"The shame..."

"The sheer horror..."

"Terribly nasty business..."

"Unthinkable consequences..."

"Everlasting dishonor!"

"The infamous rogues of history!"

"Forever cast out and away!"

"Totally and irrevocably unwanted!"

"Okay, okay, I get it," Andie said, laughing heartily. "I just thought you should know. No need to be so dramatic. I didn't know you all cared this much."

"We're your friends, haybale," Carmen said, leaning over to hug her.

The girls continued to chat about their plans while they finished getting dressed. Carmen handled everyone's makeup and Yara handled their hair. They asked Andie all sorts of questions about their new mission, but she was playing it close to the chest until they made it to the portal. She trusted them, but she didn't want to freak them out either. She hoped dearly that there wouldn't be anyone watching the portal, but the more she thought about it, the less likely it seemed.

The University was smart; they already knew that someone had been sneaking into the archives and trying to break into that room, and they would have foreseen that tonight, of all nights, would be the perfect opportunity for that person to try again-with an almost guaranteed chance of success. In addition, this *was* the portal of Scáthán Ama, the last extant portal in Noelle and perhaps the last one in the entire land of Shaeyara. Not only that, but the portal wasn't even supposed to still exist or be in the University. They couldn't afford to have that secret exposed.

Andie tried to stay calm. For better or worse, she was going to get into that room.

CHAPTER TWENTY-FIVE

AFTER ANOTHER HALF HOUR, ALL THREE GIRLS WERE ready. The trio was stunning: Andie in bronze, Carmen in red, and Yara in white. They mooned over each other for a few moments and then prepared to leave.

"You two go ahead," Andie said. "I need to do a couple things before the dance. I'll meet you there."

"Oh," Yara said, raising her eyebrows and turning from Andie to Carmen. "She needs to *do a couple things*."

"I'm sure," Carmen said. "Like Tarven. And Tarven. And a little more Tarven."

"Let's be on our way then."

The two girls moved to the door, leaving Andie blushing in the middle of the room. Yara left and Carmen was right behind her, but turned back around at the door.

"It's okay for you to have fun tonight, Andie," she said. "Everyone knows how much you care for Raesh. Even he knows it. It's a tough situation, but nobody thinks you meant to hurt him. I don't know if you two can ever be friends again, but he'll heal. In time. But tonight is about you and Tarven. Just be happy."

"Thank you, Carmen," Andie said. "I really needed to hear that. I was hoping someone would say that and I wanted it to be you. Thank you."

Carmen winked at her and disappeared. Andie waited a few minutes, until she was sure they'd had time to leave the building and make their way down the street, then she left. She hurried out of the elevator as the doors opened and in a matter of moments she was walking swiftly and determinedly toward her goal. It only took about fifteen minutes for her to reach it. Lymir's tavern.

She hadn't seen him for a while, having spent almost all of her time with Tarven, but after the conversations they'd had that night, she was sure he'd remember her. She needed to ask him a question; he was probably the only man in all of Arvall who she could trust with this and who might actually be able to answer it. The closer she got to the tavern the more careful she became, moving in shadows and searching every passing face, discreetly but carefully, to ensure her stealth. Luckily, almost everyone in downtown, midtown, or the west side between the sea and mountain. The celebration had virtually taken over the city. Andie couldn't imagine how many millions of uncia it had cost.

She arrived at the tavern and entered to find it nearly empty, as usual. Lymir was standing behind the bar and as she neared him, he seemed dumbfounded and more than a little surprised.

"Surely, ye be the girl who was in here askin' all the hard questions a fortnight ago. But the lightin split me if ye aren't not a hundred times more beautiful even now. Hearts'll be breakin' by the thousands just at the sight of ye."

Andie blushed, so hard her face began to sting.

"Thank you, Lymir."

"Don't thank me for tellin' things how they be. 'At dress suits you, girl. Its color and yours be bosom buddies."

Andie thanked him again, although for some reason she got the feeling that by "color" he hadn't meant brown hair and green eyes. But there was no way he could know that. Still, the man was truly a mystery.

"I'm sorry Lymir, I don't want to be rude or to rush you, but--"

"But time be of the essence. Ye need not explain to an old man. What's botherin' ye?"

"I know you've seen people get sucked up into the portal and leave this realm. But have you ever heard of anyone come through the portal *into* our world?"

Andie waited for his reply. Lymir seemed to be thinking hard, but Andie quickly gave up waiting; if someone had come through the portal into this realm there was no way it would be something anyone would forget. It wasn't exactly a common occurrence.

"I can't really remember, but to give ye an answer I'd say no. Not liable to be a thing even an old man would forget. Hard to tell, though. The stories 'ave been so many and so muddled, 'at they sort of blend together over time. All the same, just 'cause I never seen it doesn't mean it never happened. I'm just one man. And I'd bet my life it were more than possible. Why ye be askin' that?"

"No reason," she said, not even convincing herself.

"Girl," Lymir said, leaning toward her over the bar, "What did I tell ye the last time ye came to me wi' questions and stories? Ye're playin a dangerous game wi' powerful folk, and trust me when I say they wouldn't lose a night's sleep after watchin' ye burn for 'at curiosity. There were a time when the lust for knowledge, secret or no, were counted as a skill to be proud of. But those days are far behind."

Andie only half heeded his warning. Her mind was on the voices behind the door and their connection to the portal. Whose voices were they? Were they hurt? Where were they; here, there, some strange realm between? If she could get to the portal and open it, what could she do to help them? Could she help them?

"Thanks, Lymir," she said, turning. "I'll come back to see you when I can. I promise it won't be another two weeks."

"Now just ye hold on a moment. Rushin' like the hessian was after ye..."

Andie turned back.

"I've got somethin' for ye. Just a minute."

Lymir disappeared into the back room, leaving Andie to wait. She walked back and sat at the bar. A rotund sorcerer with the mark on his cheek turned to her and grinned. He was missing half of his teeth and the remaining half were as gray as a cold morning. He slid his hand along the bar until it was almost touching Andie.

"You look like a good time," he said in a rich tenor.

"I probably am," she replied nonchalantly.

"Tonight's the festival. What do you say to a nice long romp with ole Trisoldan? There's things I could show a pretty little thing like you."

"Come closer," she said. "Whisper some of those things in my ear."

"Oh, I'll do more than whisper."

He only managed to lean over about six inches before Andie flicked her wrist. Trisoldan was thrown thirty- five feet across the length of the entire tavern. He collided with the back wall and went halfway through it before he came to a violent stop, stuck in the wall like a barbaric and grotesque decoration.

Lymir walked back out to the bar, seemingly nonplussed.

"Well," he said, "I always knew someone would give it to 'im. Never thought a wee thing like ye would be the one. Nice work, girl."

"Sorry about the wall."

"Don't bother ye head 'bout it. I had a mind to remodel anyway. Time to class the place up a bit."

Andie smiled. She noticed he had something in his hand; it was small and glimmering. He held out his open palm to her and she saw that it was a bracelet.

"'At's white gold there. Can hardly find the stuff no more."

The bracelet was beautiful, slim, made of interwoven links shaped like leaves. No, not leaves. Scales. Like a dragon's scales. There was a small charm on the bracelet, also made of white gold, but in the shape of a sphere and on one side was an intricate stamp in the form of a dragon's head. It was incredibly subtle and would probably go unnoticed by most. There seemed to be something inside the charm and whatever it was glowed dimly. Glowing purple.

"What is it?" she asked, mesmerized as she lifted it from his hand.

"It's clear to me 'at ye've no intentions of being careful or takin' my advice. It's like ye've become hellbent on annihilation, 'erefore, ye're goin' to wear this and I'll have no arg'ments 'bout it. It's just an old family heirloom, probably offer as much protection as a popsicle, but it'd make me feel better to know ye had it. What say ye? Will ye indulge an old man?"

"Of course I'll wear it," she said, putting it on right then and there. "You sure it's just an heirloom? You seem pretty adamant to have me wear it."

She was partly nervous to ask. Lymir was an incredibly perceptive man, for all his self-deprecating jokes about being old and dull. And he had already given several hints, though certainly minor, that he knew more about her and her mission than he was letting on. Andie had come to trust him almost instantly, but that didn't change the fact that she'd only ever met the man twice and she had asked him some of the most dangerous questions possible. He was, after all, the owner of a rather sketchy and bleak tavern that served the very dregs of society in a less than reputable part of the city. Andie hadn't been nearly as careful as she should have been. And to top it all off, he'd given her a purple glowing charm with the stamp of a dragon's head on it.

"Of course, it's just mere superstition," Lymir insisted. "Like I said, probably goin' to be nothin' to ye at all, but wear it all the same, eh? Set me old mind at ease a bit."

"I won't take it off. I promise."

She smiled at him, a genuine smile of thanks and then got up to leave. She was still confused and suspicious, but she knew whatever the bracelet actually meant to him he was only trying to look out for her. He was no fool. After all the questions she'd been asking it wasn't that much of a leap to think she was off gallivanting through dangerous and secret places she had no business being. It was what she had been doing and what she was on her way to do at that very moment.

As she headed for SKY 6, Andie noticed that the bracelet felt weird. No, not weird, good. She held up her wrist to check it. The purple glow made her wonder. Could it be dragon magic? Whatever was inside of it was very dim, almost extinguished. She couldn't tell exactly what it was, but she knew it was magic. That much was clear.

CHAPTER TWENTY-SIX

As always, Andie was able to relax on SKY 6. The train was traveling somewhat slower that night and whether it was to show off the views of Arvall City and Brie Mountain or the amenities of the train itself, Andie didn't know. Every seat on the train was taken, filled with the sleek silver tuxedos or luminous, pearlescent ball gowns of people who looked far too wealthy to be sitting in coach. Andie felt strangely at ease among them; they were rich and thrilled, and she knew that they would leave her to herself.

She was becoming nervous about her mission. She knew she could trust Yara and Carmen, and she knew that when the moment came for her to reveal to them exactly what they had signed up for, they would follow her into danger. She also knew that despite Lymir's claims to ignorance and superstition he was a wise man, and the charm bracelet he'd given her was somehow meant to protect her. The other thing she knew was that she had an even wider network of people looking out for her. There was Marvo who—human or not—would give his dying breath to help her. There was also Tarven, the boy who'd changed her life. Despite all his secrets there was no doubt in her mind that he would come to her if push came to shove. Even her father back in Michaelson would risk everything just to be able to protect her for a single moment. And Raesh. Warm, sweet, loyal Raesh, who would never let so small a thing as jealousy keep him from her.

Andie's concern now was moving more toward what would happen to that network of friends. She wasn't without her own sense of self-preservation, but she'd long since come to terms with the realization that she was probably going to die. Lymir was right: she was playing the game, but without knowing the rules or who the other players were. And the University had hundreds of years of murder under its belt. Every day she walked into that black marble structure, she knew it might be the last. But that was for herself. If anything were to happen to the people she cherished—the people who believed in her enough to follow her—she hoped that she would die first because she would never be able to forgive herself.

SKY 6 reached the University and the passengers began to unload, more than a few of them were already reeling from wine and whatever else they'd been ingesting on the way up. As soon as the mountain altitude hit some of them, they collapsed into heaving piles. Andie skirted the chaos and went inside. It was a struggle to navigate the halls as almost all of the University's six hundred thousand students were in attendance. There were also the faculty, visitors, and important figures from around the world. Andie fought hard for every step, with perhaps a hundred "Excuse me's" and "Sorry's." Things petered out some when she finally reached the end of the hall and was under the endless void. The ethereal glow of the marble was even more magnificent than usual and even after her many months there, Andie still didn't know where the light came from.

To reach the Grand Mirror Hall of Terpsichore, Andie had to venture down a new hallway. There was no hope of getting lost though, for the closer she got to the ballroom, the more the smell of the mixed fuil glas and anáil fuar filled her body. She knew immediately it had been a success. How could it not be? There were simply no words for the smell and as she turned the corner and entered the room she was nearly bowled over by the sight. The entire upper halves of the walls were covered with the mixed species, which Tarven had named anáil saol. The new species was cerulean and forest, brilliant in the University's glow and strong in the greatest way. Andie couldn't help but feel a swell of pride.

She felt prouder still when she noticed that several eyes were watching her make her entrance and more were turning by the second. She walked slowly, trying to affect some grace if it were possible, smiling that beautiful smile that had won so many hearts in her favor. People were whispering as she passed by and from their expressions, Andie knew they were impressed. She kept talking to herself to stay calm. "Don't fall." "Head high." "Remember to thank Carmen for this dress." "Find Tarven." People began to smile and nod at her. She nodded back, queenly for a girl not used to the spotlight. For once in her life, she had some true conception of her beauty.

As she was thinking his name, she saw his face. Tarven was standing in the middle of the room, his arm already up and waiting for her as if he'd known where she was all along. He'd decided to skip tradition and wear a dark blue tuxedo with a black shirt and tie. He did, however, opt for one of the traditional hairstyles. He looked exceptionally handsome. Perfect. She walked up to him and took his arm.

'Hi," she said. "I feel like all of Arvall's watching me. I guess with so many foreign dignitaries all the world is watching."

"Well, you're the most beautiful woman breathing. And now the whole world knows it."

It was the perfect thing to say.

Tarven led her up the stone steps onto the main level of the mirror room where the dancing would be. Andie looked around and saw that the board had formed the room to look like one of the great ballrooms of Hightowyr. Three rooms, in fact. Now that Andie had reached the main level, she could see that the room had been thought into an additional grand ballroom on either side. Tarven held her hand and they walked over to a fountain that had to be at least fifty feet tall. Andie was surprised to see people holding their cups beneath the stream.

"Am I seeing things or are those rich people drinking the water from the fountain?" Andie asked.

"It's not water, silly. Of course, we call it fountain water, but it's actually a kind of wine made from the recipe of the Terpsichore founding family. It's only made during the time of the Winter Festival."

"And they couldn't think of a better name than 'fountain water?'"

"Its proper name is *comhlacht bunaitheach*, but I suppose that was a bit of a mouthful."

The voice belonged to a young-looking man dressed in the traditional silver tux and holding a champagne flute of the fountain water. He had a smile that made one trust him instantly, but wasn't arrogant or pompous in the least.

"Where are your manners, Tarven?" he asked,

grinning. "Introduce me to this beautiful lady who seems to have gotten drunk and accidentally fallen into your company."

Andie smiled and blushed for the third time that night.

"This is my date, Andie Rogers. And this, Andie, is one of my professors, Marcus Iceubes, professor of folklore."

"I resent that," Marcus said, shaking Andie's hand.

"Well, you are."

"True, but that makes me sound so boring and narrow. I want to be exciting."

"Well, you did introduce yourself with a historical anecdote."

"Hm. Fair."

"It's a pleasure to meet you," Andie said, taken with him immediately.

"Not quite. You have to try this very, very old wine first."

He turned to pick something up. It was a glass figure shaped like a funny sphere. Andie looked closer and saw that it was a palm-sized miniature of earth with a snowflake perched on top. Marcus handed it to Andie, shaking his head as if embarrassed on behalf of whoever had crafted it.

"You never know what they're going to do with the spellglass from year to year," he said. "How about a champagne flute?"

He looked at the spellglass and it formed itself into a frosted champagne flute to match his own.

"Thanks, but I think a brandy glass will do," Andie said. "You know, country girl and all."

Instantly, the spellglass shrunk and widened to become a brandy glass. Andie thought for a moment then decided to manifest a panorama of a snowstorm along the sides.

"Oh, I see we have a show off among us," Marcus said. "Welcome home."

He led her and Tarven to the fountain and Andie held the glass under the stream. Marcus handed her a napkin and she wiped the side. She took one sip of it and from the look on her face, they knew she'd never tasted anything so delicious. She downed the glass and reached for more.

"Oh, I like you," Marcus said.

TARVEN LED Andie around the crowd and introduced her to some faculty members and professors, as was customary for anyone working at the University who brought a date. Andie also met the provost, an old woman with kind eyes and the air of someone who never intended to die. She spent the greater part of the evening with Tarven. Marcus popped in occasionally and kept them from the boredom that was the introductory phase of the celebration. Still, Andie couldn't stop herself from getting anxious. It was getting later and later, and she was no longer sure she would have a chance to get away. Every time she tried to excuse herself, someone started a conversation with her. She was flattered by all their attentions, but she had somewhere to be. If it wasn't other people, it was Tarven. He really was trying to be a terrific date—and he was succeeding—but he never let her get more than a few feet away.

Finally, she managed to get Tarven deep into conversation with three young men who'd tried to talk to her. She was slowly slipping away when Carmen and Yara found her.

"Come on," Yara said. "Girl time."

"Definitely," Carmen added, in that accept-this-as-your-circumstance way of hers. "We'll have her back soon enough for you to dance her off her feet."

"Or whatever you were planning on doing to her," Yara mumbled devilishly.

"But I've not had my chance yet."

It was Professor Harrock. Andie nearly sighed in despair, but he was actually one of her favorite instructors. He held out his hand, like the shiest, but most determined gentleman on earth, and she accepted.

"After this one," she said to the girls.

They walked out to the middle of the dance floor. Andie wanted desperately to be investigating the secrets of the archives, but she knew she could last one more dance. She gave Professor Harrock a genuine smile and tried not to laugh when Marcus put on a face of exaggerated sympathy across the room. Andie prepared herself for another sweet, but mundane dance. But she was greatly shocked when he pulled her in close, all the way against him and whispered in her ear.

"So, you think your magic protects you?"

"What?"

"You think no one can see who you are or know what you're doing. You think you've outsmarted an institution that has enslaved or destroyed every enemy to cross its path in the last five hundred years. You think you're powerful. Special."

Andie tried to pull away, but Professor Harrock was strong, much stronger than he looked. Much stronger than he should have been. She tried to release magic into his arm from her hand, but it didn't seem to have an effect.

"You've been putting that pretty little nose where it doesn't belong. You think we're oblivious because you meddled with your icon, but we know everything you've been up to since you first sunk it into your palm."

"That's impossible."

"Is it? Who do you think allowed that so-called spell to reach the students? We wanted you all to think that we weren't watching you and like dumb sheep every last one of you believed yourself free."

"You're a villain. I don't know what's going on here, but I'll-"

"You'll mind your tongue or I'll rip it out and send it home to your cripple of a father. You've been warned. The dragons and everything they spawned is off limits, and by off limits I mean on pain of death. I do not fear death and thus I deal it willingly. You're beautiful and brilliant, maybe even stronger than we think, but we will lay waste to you and every inch of the nineteen years of your life. Everything. Everyone. Even Tarven."

"You won't touch him."

"Touch him? Stupid girl. We've already done more than that. Look at him."

Andie started to turn her head and then stopped. She didn't want to give him the satisfaction.

"Look at him or I'll burn your friends in their beds tonight."

Andie tried to think of a way out, an escape, but couldn't. She wouldn't risk her friend's lives for her own pride. She turned and looked for Tarven. He was already watching her. As soon as he caught her eye, he tried to smile and look excited, but she'd already seen the truth on his face. He knew what Professor Harrock was doing. He was a part of it.

"See, we took him and made him ours. That's what we do. We corrupt for the sake of purification. One more thing. Stay away from the portal. We'll know if you go near it again."

Professor Harrock let go of her and stepped away. He bowed, smiling, and then left. Andie made her way back to Tarven, not because she wanted to see him, but because she didn't yet know where else to move to.

"Are you okay?" Tarven asked, in full cover-up mode. "Come here. What was Professor Harrock talking about?"

"Nothing," she said. "It was just about some research I was doing. He says it won't be... suitable for my final essay. Excuse me, I need some air."

She left. She couldn't look at him anymore and it took every ounce of her strength not to vaporize him where he stood.

CHAPTER TWENTY-SEVEN

ON HER WAY OUT, ANDIE FOUND HERSELF WALKING
between Carmen and Yara. She didn't know if she'd
found them or they found her, but she felt a surge of
strength the moment she knew they were beside her.
They never stopped walking, just left the grand mirror
room side by side, three young women with a secret
purpose.

Andie moved differently then. With purpose. She'd
heard everything Professor Harrock had said and she
was afraid—she *knew* she was afraid—but she couldn't
stop. She had to open the door, touch that portal, save
those voices. Consequences or no. Yara and Carmen
moved silently beside her, giving her a kind of fortitude
as they weaved through the crowded halls in the
direction of Leabherlann. Andie couldn't lie to herself:
She was playing fast and loose with their lives. She'd

been told, explicitly, only moments ago, that if she continued to look into these things she would be condemning everyone in her life. Truth be told, she hadn't yet decided what to do and she knew she had until they reached the archives to decide. It was coming to the point where she would have to decide between saving the voices in the portal and saving the living bodies around her.

They reached Leabherlann and Andie taught Yara and Carmen the spell that allowed them to pass through the door. Once inside, Andie made straight for the archives without a word. How would she tell them their lives were in danger? How would she tell them the University had been watching them ever since they put the icon in? How would she handle their fear? She began to move quicker and with more focus, perhaps driven somewhat crazed by the sheer weight of the moment that waited ahead. Leabherlann was totally empty, not a soul apart from the three of them, and their footsteps echoed like sharp yelps in the great darkness. As they neared the archive, Andie could hear Carmen's footsteps slowing, lightening, the fire going out of the girl as she realized where they were heading. Yara seemed less apprehensive, but Andie could hear the change in her footsteps, as well. At last they descended the short staircase to the lower level and stood facing the entrance to the hallway, beyond which lay the archives and the door that hid the portal, Andie turned to face them.

"If you go into this room with me your lives will be in danger," she said. "After that, the chances of things returning to normal for you are pretty slim."

"As in our lives are completely screwed if we take one more step," Yara said.

"Exactly."

Yara took a step back and collapsed against the wall. Carmen stood bewildered and mute, gazing around her as if she didn't know which way to turn.

"There's more." Andie said. "They're monitoring us, right now. They have been since we put the icons in. The dampening spell never worked. They only wanted us to think it did. They've known everything we've done since we inserted it. I'm still not sure exactly who we're up against or what is going on here, but Professor Harrock is in on it. He just threatened me on the dance floor. He basically said that anyone I care about will be killed if I continue. I don't know if I'm going in yet or not, but you two need to turn back."

"Turn back?" Carmen asked.

"Now. For all I know they're already planning our deaths and I won't have the two of you on my conscious. You've been too good to me."

"Who do you think you are?" asked Carmen, staring at Andie with utter fury. "Do you think the world revolves around you? That you can just... just take what you want when you want without consequences? Do you think you get to make all the decisions for the rest of us? Beg for our help one minute and turn us away the next? Do you think we didn't understand what you wanted? Do you think we're stupid, or blind, or foolish? You don't control us."

"You never will," Yara said. "You asked us to come with you because you trusted us and you needed us. I cast an augmentation spell on myself earlier tonight. Like I do every year. I make it so that I can hear a conversation a hundred yards away because I like to know what the foreigners think of Arvall. I heard virtually every word of Harrock's poison. I heard what he told you to do, the things he threatened he'd do, and yet here I am. I told Carmen and yet there she is."

"We're your friends, Andie," Carmen said, standing straighter then than Andie could remember. "Danger or no. Don't insult us by trying to push us away when you so clearly need us with you."

Andie simply nodded. She was so happy she could have collapsed against them there.

"Besides," Carmen added, "If they've really been watching us since we first got our icons, I expect they've already gotten quite an eyeful from me."

"They'll be long dead before they finish sorting out my perversions and crimes," Yara said with a smile.

The three girls shared a smile. Andie turned and faced the hallway. There was no point in hiding now.

She raised her hand and with her mind began to disassemble the magic of the hallway. She'd grown strong and the handful of defensive spells were no good. It had been a long while since she'd doubted her own sanity, but she had a wavering moment then. There was just something about her circumstance that night that felt at odds with what it should be. She didn't have time to worry about that then, though. The three girls moved swiftly down the hallway and walked as a unit through the archives. Yara and Carmen gazed up and across at all the strange and ancient volumes. Andie had seen it all before.

They neared the door and this time not only were the voices louder, more painful, but Andie could feel the magic of the door before they were even close to it. They'd done something to enhance the magic and whatever it was had intensified the voices as well. But as Andie struggled to stay on her feet and focus her mind, Carmen and Yara seemed completely unbothered. She could tell by the orientation of their bodies that they felt the magic, but they couldn't hear the voices. Then Andie remembered: Tarven couldn't hear them either. Maybe only the dragonborn could hear them.

"Andie, what's wrong?" Carmen asked.

"The voices. They're too loud. I can't... I can't..."

"Just tell us what to do."

"You have to get that door open."

Carmen and Yara approached the door, wary. Andie

239

sank to her knees, unable to think or move. Carmen and Yara seemed to be arguing over something. They both tried a spell on the door and when nothing worked, they began to alternate, giving the door everything they had. With every failure, the voices grew in Andie's head; her bones began to ache and blood was coming from her ears.

"You have to open it!" she screamed, desperate.

Yara was holding her head, wracking her brain for something while Carmen tried spells, charms, incantations, and even hexes. Suddenly Yara's eyes leapt open and she grabbed Carmen. Yara said something to her and then they both kneeled down in front of Andie. They grabbed her under her arms and drug her over to the door. Carmen took Andie's bloody hands from her ears and placed them on the door, then she and Yara both placed their hands on the door. They began to chant as Andie began to swoon. Louder and louder the girls became, and lower and lower the voices went. Soon the whispers that had once been screams were fading into nothing as the magic flowed out of the door and into the three girls. The sorcerer's magic felt odd against Andie's flesh, but anything was better than the voices.

"Andie, you're bleeding," Yara said. "Maybe we should go."

"No," Andie said, louder than she meant to. "I'll be fine. There are worse injuries. I didn't come all this way and go through all that to leave without having some of my questions answered."

She wasn't lying; her dragon blood had begun to heal her instantly. In a matter of moments she would be fine.

With her friends' help, Andie rose to her feet and stepped forward to the door. Carefully, with the gravity of everything she'd suffered on her shoulders, Andie pushed the door open. It was like nothing she could have imagined. The room is massive, obviously spelled to seem smaller from the outside. It was made entirely of blue stone, which was said to have magical properties, but Andie had never seen it before. The room was so huge it seemed that it must have been bigger than the archives, bigger than Leabherlann itself. In the center of the space was an enormous circular pool bordered by yet another kind of stone; on the stone were carved symbols that Andie couldn't decipher. There was a mist, heavier and more nerve-wracking than any natural mist, hanging about.

The voices suddenly came back again, but now only as whispers. As the three young sorceresses neared the pool, Andie could hear a multitude of fleeting cries rising from the pool. Andie hurried forward, despite herself.

"I don't believe it," Carmen said.

"This is impossible," said Yara. "This shouldn't even be here. It shouldn't even exist. It's just a legend."

"Hello!" Andie said, leaning over the pool. "Hello! Can you hear me? Tell me how to help you! I'm here to save you!"

"Andie, I meant what I said, I'd follow you anywhere, but maybe we should take a minute to think this through," Yara cautioned. "If this portal is real, then maybe the legends are, too."

"You mean the terrifying stories?" said Carmen. "The ones where a few kids mysteriously go missing every few years, never to be heard from again? Or the ones where entire nations waged war just to look at this thing? Nothing good can come of that thing."

But Andie was beyond them. Leaning far over the pool and peering inside, she could see them. The people. *Her* people. The dragonborn were there, with their colorful hair, iridescent eyes, and dragon scale armor. There, too, were dragons—great magnificent beasts larger and more beautiful than imagination, stunning beyond description. One of the people looked up, straight up and into Andie's eyes.

"Help us," he called weakly.

It was in that moment that Andie knew her dreams were real. All of them.

"Carmen, Yara, they're in danger. We have to help them."

"Who?" they asked simultaneously.

Andie beckoned them over to the pool. At first, they

didn't seem to see anything, but when she saw their eyes go wide she knew they finally saw.

"I see them!" Yara said.

"Yeah," said Carmen. "And I can hear them, too!"

"Good," Andie said. "Because this is the only opportunity we'll ever get to save them."

CHAPTER TWENTY-EIGHT

CARMEN AND YARA TOOK A MOMENT, CLEARLY STILL not fully believing. Maybe they couldn't believe it was real or maybe they couldn't believe it was happening to them, but Andie couldn't afford to give them the time they needed to process. And neither could her people.

"Carmen, Yara, I need you to guard this room," she said. "We know they're watching us and we know they mean to stop us. I need you now. All my people need you."

The two girls looked at each other and then at Andie.

"We'll do everything we can," Carmen said.

She and Yara hurried back over to the door and stood guard. They began to slowly wave their hands in front of themselves, the fingers beginning to glow as they closed the door and cast enchantments across it.

Andie turned back to the pool and leaned over it as far as she could without falling in. As Carmen and Yara chanted into the hallway behind her, Andie called into the pool below. It seemed as if they could hardly hear her and only intermittently, as if she were some radio signal that couldn't come through clearly. She could see them turn their faces up every now and then, responding to some clip of her voice that had fought its way through. She couldn't hear them either, try as she might, and she nearly fell in twice trying to put her face close enough to the pool to make sense of the rising murmurs. Then she got an idea. She remembered how she'd released her dragon essence in Leabherlann. Astral projection had allowed her spirit to be free in order to accomplish tasks her mind could not; it wouldn't be necessary to go full spirit, just enough to get a certain degree of distance between body and spirit. She released the smallest part of herself, enough to connect with the visions in the pool, but not so much that she lost the effective use of her corporeal body. She existed then in two states simultaneously.

"Help us, please!" one woman cried.

"Time is running out!" said another.

Andie's projection allowed her to see beyond the women to the mountain. Covering every inch of the peak that she could see were her people, frightened, breathless, unable to move for lack of anywhere to run to. Husbands were cradling their wives, who were in turn cradling their children. Suddenly their numbers and suffering were laid out before Andie in a vast panorama of misfortune. And then she saw it: the spell rolling across the land that was so massive it took up all the space between land and sky. On and on it came, relentless, inevitable, a storm of violent magic unlike anything ever seen on earth and as purple as the deepest heart of lavender. It was so close, unbelievably close, and it was destroying everything it touched. If the dragonborn couldn't escape, their entire race would be finished. And what would that mean for their descendants?

Then Andie saw her, looking up from the portal and speaking to her. The woman seemed calmer than the rest, as if she had decided on a course of peace. She was standing on the forward-most precipice of the mountain and she was so beautiful the word must have been created for her. She gazed up at Andie like a mother gazing at her child and, amazingly, despite the destruction and fear surrounding her, the woman was smiling. Andie knew the smile was for her, to calm her down so she could focus and help them. She focused on the woman.

"Tell me what to do," Andie said. "I'll do anything."

"What is your name?" the woman asked.

"Andie."

"It is my honor, Andie. I am called Saeryn. All you need to do is focus on the dragon magic inside of you."

"How did you know-"

"Only a dragonborn could have heard my calls. And only a dragonborn can save us. Just focus on the magic that is already inside of you, deep within, in the very paoum of your soul. Let those deeper parts of yourself guide you. Your spirit and instincts already know what to do."

Andie felt the anxiety and fear like a thousand tons of cold pressure on her chest. She turned to look at Carmen and Yara—now done casting enchantments and patiently standing guard. They had no idea she was one of the dragonborn. She loved them and trusted them, but she'd never asked them how they felt about dragons and the race they created. What if they feared her? What if they couldn't accept her? What if they tried to kill her?

"I can't," she said. "It's too dangerous."

"Be brave, Andie. Fear alone is the great danger. Only you can pull us through and when you do we will protect you. There will be nothing on Earth that can harm you. Our moments here in our own time are diminishing. We cannot stay here a minute longer, you must bring us through to your time."

Necessity had taken her choice from her and now all Andie had left was her duty to her people. She closed her eyes and dropped the veil of her disguise. She returned to the brilliant, luminous truth of her heritage and she was more beautiful than can be described. But just as she dropped the veil, there was a massive explosion on the other side of the door. The blast jolted all three girls and Andie's projection snapped back home as Carmen and Yara stumbled against the pillars.

"What was that?" Yara screamed.

"Andie, I think we're going to have to-"

But as Carmen turned and saw Andie she stopped short. Yara saw her, too. There was a long silence while Andie grew tense, watching her friends watch her and waiting for some reaction, any indication at all of how they truly felt. And then, like a light in the darkness, Yara laughed.

"I knew it!" she said. "I'd been suspecting for months, but I knew it! All your questions and research and mystery. All those items you tried to find and your secrecy about your mother and your family. I knew it, I knew you were dragonborn."

"Is that okay?" Andie asked.

"Are you kidding? It's awesome. You're my friend, Andie, I'll take you as you are."

They smiled at each other. Andie turned to Carmen, who was still staring slack-jawed.

"And you?" Andie asked.

"Why didn't you tell me?"

"I was scared and I didn't know if you would be afraid. Or, kill me, if we're speaking truthfully."

Carmen simply stared. Just then another explosion shook the entire room and several of the huge chandeliers fell from the ceiling. They were running out of time and in more ways than one. Carmen ran over to Andie and hugged her. The embrace said so much that nothing else was necessary.

"You and I are going to talk about this later," Carmen said. "But right now, we need to do what we came here for."

"What's on the other side of that door?" Andie asked.

Another explosion boomed through the hall and this one caused cracks to spread through the entire wall. Whatever or whoever was outside would be inside soon enough. Carmen and Yara waved their hands again and sealed the cracks in the wall, but they knew time was short. Now they could hear shouting on the other side of the door. Andie recast her partial projection. It allowed her to see through the door as if nothing were there: on the other side were several professors, hooded monitors —the University's security—and Tarven. So, finally, he'd chosen a side. Fortunately, there were no Searchers or guns, which would have meant a sure and painful death. At least now maybe they had a chance, however slight. Andie couldn't help herself: she wished Raesh were there.

"Andie, you must hurry."

It was Saeryn calling from the pool. Carmen and Yara, understanding, hurried back to the wall and pushed with all of their magic to protect it, yet there was no way the two of them could stand long against the power on the other side of the wall. Andie ran back to the pool and took a deep breath. She turned her spirit inside, into her blood. She'd held herself back for so long that to release her full ability again would take real effort. She searched and reached deep down into the magic she hadn't disturbed since she was a child. Since her mother was taken. It was obvious the magic was there, but perhaps it had been dormant too long. No. There it was, curled and slumbering like the great beasts from which it came. She reached for it, almost had it in her grasp, when an explosion ripped the room asunder. Carmen and Yara were thrown back several feet and Andie was blasted into one of the pillars. The explosion was so powerful that it split the room in two across the ceiling. Only the strength of the mountain and the pillars interspersed throughout the room kept it all from collapsing.

Through the rip where the door used to be came Professor Harrock, Tarven, and all the others. Their faces were full of rage.

CHAPTER TWENTY-NINE

ANDIE GOT UP, SLOWER THAN SHE MEANT TO, BUT IT felt as if some of her ribs might be broken. The dragon magic was kicking in to help heal her, but before she could say a word or even get all the way back on her feet, one of the apoplectic professors threw a lightning bolt at her. It came faster than sound and more blinding than a flash of the sun. It hit Andie before she even knew it had been cast and knocked her even further back. This time she didn't try to get up.

"Tarven," she called from where she lay, "Help us."

"There's no help for you now, Andie," he said. "Just lie there. Maybe this can be over quickly."

Andie tried to raise herself up, just to her knees, but even the dragon magic couldn't heal those wounds so fast.

"Why?" she asked. "What could possibly make you so evil?"

"Why does it matter? I've been with them for years, before I ever even met you. There was never even a chance for you. I studied you and memorized your history before you set foot in Arvall City. We knew who you were when you applied to the University. Do you really think the University doesn't keep a record of the people they've killed? When they took your mother, they marked your family for surveillance. You and your father were never alone in Michaelson. I bet you think what happened to him was an accident."

Andie almost stopped breathing.

"That's impossible. It *was* an accident."

"It was made to look like one. They were never going to let you go. The only reason you lived this long is because they were curious about their own security. They only let you live to test the weaknesses of their own system. Your entire life was an experiment."

"And a very successful one," said a new voice.

Andie recognized it instantly. It was the voice she'd heard talking with Tarven that night in Leabherlann. And now she knew why his voice sounded familiar. It was Myamar Mharú, chancellor of western Noelle. Andie had only ever seen him once before; he gave a speech at the University around the beginning of the year. Still, Andie could hardly focus on him or anything else. She was heartbroken to know that Tarven had betrayed her so absolutely. She'd always known something was off, always had her suspicions. She even caught him in the middle of one or two blatant lies, but she'd never suspected that his deception ran this deep, that his disdain for her and everything she was could be so huge. But she had to focus. Tarven had made his decision and now she had to make hers. She had people to save, and now that included Carmen and Yara. Tarven stepped forward. He reached inside his tuxedo jacket and removed a small bronze and black plant in a tiny pot. Decepticatus.

"Remember this little guy?" Tarven taunted. "I'm surprised you didn't guess from the name, but they feed on human lies. The day you saw him leaning toward me was because I was lying to you. Idiot. Now, let's see what you have to say. Do you know where any other dragonborn are?"

"No," Andie said through gritted teeth.

The plant leaned toward her.

"Is your father fully disabled?"

"Yes."

"Have you found any books in Leabherlann with information you shouldn't have?"

Andie paused for a moment, trying to make herself believe her words.

"No."

The little bronze plant leaned further toward Andie and waved its limbs.

"Lie number two," Tarven said. "Do you have the means of opening this portal?"

"No."

The plant leaned over even more and waved a little harder.

"Lie number three. Are there any dragons that are still alive?"

"No."

The plant leaned even more and Andie was ashamed.

"Hm."

The power of the dragons that ran through her blood had healed her enough to stand and without thinking she pushed herself to her feet with magic. No one was expecting it. Andie raised her hands and slammed them down against the floor; a wave of energy rippled out across it, cracking the stones and flinging the men as it went. She waved her hands and erected a shield before her. Her spells could go out, but theirs couldn't get in. Before anyone had time to think, spells were flying back and forth everywhere in a kind of crazed firework show. Stone exploded into dust in the air as wildly aimed spells missed their mark and collided with the walls and pillars. Andie moved like water, casting counter charms faster than ever before. She ducked and slid to safety as one of the professors held his throat and breathed fire. Andie gripped him with magic and fused his body with a stone pillar. He struggled, but couldn't pull away. He wouldn't be bothering her for a while. She hadn't even fully understood how she did what she did to him. Tarven was across the room, behind Professor Harrock, pretending to be fierce, but really just hiding. He never was very good at casting.

"What's wrong with you people?" Andie screamed, taking shelter behind a pillar while she regrouped. "If you don't let me get to that portal, an entire race of people will die! Don't you understand that? All my people will be dead!"

"It's really for the best," came Professor Harrock's condescending voice. "The dragonborn are a threat and a plague. If you honestly think we would risk allowing them to be free in our time, then you haven't been paying attention. They *will* die tonight. And only time will tell if you die before or after that portal is a pile of ash. If your race goes extinct in history...Well, let's just say it doesn't bode well for those of you still around today. There's no escape, no resistance, no hope. You can only-"

Andie heard Professor Harrock give a grunt and then she heard a heavy thump. She peaked around the pillar and saw him on his knees. He seemed to have fallen there and he was clutching his chest. When his hands dropped, Andie could see that his chest had been shot through and a hole was left straight in the middle, next to his heart. He fell forward head first, unconscious or dead, Andie couldn't tell. Andie froze in a daze and held

255

her hand to her mouth in shock, holding in a scream, as she stared at his body lying still on the floor. She was quickly brought back to reality as she heard crashes and bangs around her, spells flying this way and that. What was this coming to? She looked around as she cast spells, trying to see where the attack had come from. She saw Yara still lying unconscious near the door, but Carmen had her hand up and extended in Harrock's direction, as if just finished casting a spell. One of the other professors tried to bring a pillar down on her, but Carmen shielded herself and the part of the pillar that touched her vanished into particles.

"Carmen, over here!" Andie shouted.

Carmen got to her feet, trying to defend herself from the barrage of spells.

"What about Yara?" she asked.

Andie strengthened her shield and then stepped out into the floor. She flicked her wrist and Yara's body snapped over into her arms. She returned to her shelter and moments later Carmen joined her. Carmen worked on trying to revive Yara while Andie cast retaliation spells. She caught one professor right in the face and the woman fell instantly, taken by the purple flames.

"Your kind are destroyers," Mharú's voice said. "You cannot be allowed to survive."

"We're destroyers?" she responded, incredulous. "You're the ones who've been hunting us for centuries. You're the ones who slaughtered the dragons. It was you and all the people like you who made sure that the reign of terror lasted all these centuries without any hope or quarter for my people. Don't talk to me about destroyers!"

"We are the rightful rulers of this land! The dragonborn had their chance and they were too weak to withstand! They were insects compared to us!"

"Is that why you were so scared? Why you're still terrified that one day they could come back? What did the dragonborn ever do to you? To anybody? What was it about them and the dragons that just seemed so dangerous and so insurmountable that you people had to slaughter them continuously without remorse?"

"They existed."

And that was enough. Andie had had enough.

Andie was growing more and more furious: with the sorcerers, with the plight of her people, with the threats and the hatred and the fact that Carmen still couldn't wake Yara. Andie stood and released a wave of magic that ran hot and rapid through the room. She erected a second shield, but this one stretched from floor to ceiling and ensured a safe path to the portal. The professors continued to cast at the shield, but to no effect. Andie ran to the portal and prepared to project.

"Carmen, don't worry about Yara just now. You can cast spells from behind the shield. Give me as much time as you can."

Carmen nodded and gently laid Yara down. She rose

and took a stance behind the shield, beginning to cast with a stunning ferocity. Andie projected again, this time drawing on the core of her magic, and found a multitude of spells suddenly appearing in her mind. Without questioning it, she began to recite them over the portal with her eyes closed. She followed Saeryn's words and simply trusted the history and power in her own blood. Soon she could hear Saeryn below, chanting along with her. Then all the people began to join in. It felt good to give in, to be one with her people, but the spell was powerful. So powerful. Andie wasn't used to this: channeling so much magic, doing a spell with others, pulling on the very root of her dragon magic. It began to overwhelm her almost immediately and the more she pushed herself, the harder it became.

Behind her, Carmen was fighting with everything inside her. The shield was beginning to fail as Andie lost strength and cracks and holes began to appear in the soft light of the barrier. Carmen continued to cast, fierce and unstoppable as ever. Andie was feeling weak now, weak enough to want to lay down, but she kept pushing and reaching and reciting. Her head began to droop and her sense began to go, but she kept reciting. She began to bleed again and the dragon magic within her stopped healing, but she kept reciting. She fell to her knees, but she kept reciting.

"Please," she thought. "Just let me have the strength to do this one thing." But she continued to weaken.

Against her own wishes, she began to lose hope. She could barely hold herself up and the shield was almost down. Maybe this was it. Maybe this was the end of everything.

But just as she was growing faithless, there was a blast near the door. Andie had just enough strength to turn her face in that direction. A group of people in black came rushing in, tight, quick, and casting spells as if they were born to it. And at the head of the group were Raesh and Marvo.

CHAPTER THIRTY

Raesh cast a spell at the nearest professor and when it left his body on its trajectory it looked like a bolt of light with a hundred whipping tails, twisting furiously as it shot across the room and sent the professor soaring so far up and away in the cavernous room that Andie lost track of him. Raesh had said his magic was unpredictable and now she saw what he meant. He cast again and again and again, making his way across the room to Carmen. The others with him were casting rapidly as well, and the professors were finally starting to understand there was a chance the tide could turn against them.

Marvo was the only one not casting and that was because he had a gun; not the unpredictable, blood fueled weapons of modern-age Noelle, but one of the Old-World weapons. Every time he shot it, the barrel flashed and boomed. Unlike the spells that were flying wild, the gun was deadly accurate and Marvo knew how to use it. The professors had to erect shields of their own to protect themselves from him.

Tarven, whether out of his extreme cowardice or premeditated feint, launched an attack on the newcomers from behind. They hadn't seen him when they came into the room and he was taking full advantage of it. He took down two of the newcomers with a few snaps of his wrists and then he reached in his coat and pulled out the new plant species he and Andie had bred together. He waved his hand in front of the blooms and extracted the liquid from the plant. He threw it into the faces of three of the newcomers and they began to choke and shrivel. Soon their faces were smoking and they dropped to the floor, bodies limp before they even touched the ground. Andie couldn't believe it. There was a mirror room full of people dancing under thousands of those flowers.

"You'll pay for this," she said in his direction, weakly.

"Not before I see you dead," he said back to her.

Tarven disappeared behind a pillar and Marvo fired off a couple rounds while making his way to Andie.

"What are you doing here?" she asked.

"Well, what a fine way to say thank you," he said, digging for something in his pocket. "Let's just call it a rescue mission. Unless of course you don't need us?"

"But how did you know? How did you find us?"

"Andie, I promised your father I would watch over you. He never told me you were dragonborn, but I'm no fool. I knew your mother was and I always suspected she passed on the gene. I've kept a closer watch on you since you've been in Arvall than I ever have on anyone else, even Raesh. You're important to me. But to answer your question, when you split up from Carmen earlier tonight she called Raesh and told him she thought you were up to something dangerous. This isn't the first time she's called us about you, but like every other time we got ready just in case. When she didn't call us back to say it was a false alarm, we came. Of course, with the festival going on, it was the perfect cover to get into the University and it didn't take a genius to figure out where you'd be."

He stood up to take a few more shots and then kneeled down again. He found something in his pocket and gave it to Andie.

"Here. Drink this and don't waste time asking me what it is."

Without hesitation, Andie turned the vial up and drank every drop of the liquid. She couldn't describe the effect other than to say that it put a fire in her. It didn't heal her, but it dampened the pain so that she could hardly feel it.

"I have to be honest," Marvo said, still shooting,

"You've looked better. Can you finish what you started?"

"I don't have a choice," she said.

Andie pushed her fists against the ground and gained her feet. She leaned over the portal again and projected.

"Can you hold them off?" she asked Marvo.

"I was born for it," he said, cocking the gun and moving with a dexterity she wouldn't have thought he had.

Andie went back to chanting as the spells and gunshots flew around her. Marvo and the newcomers were strong and more than able to hold their own against the professors. Andie's shield had fallen, but Carmen had erected a new one. Andie felt a hand on her shoulder and realized that Carmen was standing behind her, one hand on Andie and another hand casting angrily. Andie felt stronger just having her there.

Across the room, Raesh was unleashing his magic like a madman. His magic was unpredictable and by the look on his face you could tell he didn't always cast the spell he meant to, but he was a terrible force in that room. He guarded Yara's body fiercely. Marvo couldn't shoot the professors now that they had shields, but his incredible aim kept them from getting too close or going anywhere he didn't want them to. The newcomers, whoever they were, were expert sorcerers and sorceresses. They were relentless, unafraid, powerful.

The professors were as arrogant and destructive as ever, but they grew desperate. They tried to bring down the pillars and even some spots of the wall to kill their opponents. They fought with no decency and no shame.

Andie felt numb, weak, cold, but she didn't stop chanting this time. Saeryn and her people below were doing their part and it was Andie's duty to do hers. Everyone around her was fighting with all they had. She couldn't do any less. Suddenly someone was kneeling beside her.

"Andie."

It was Raesh. Andie couldn't stop chanting, but she felt a wave of relief wash over her. She was happy he was there beside her.

"Andie, what were you thinking? How could you come in here with just Carmen and Yara, without even knowing what you're doing, without even having other people who know where you are? You could've been killed! You could've gotten them killed!"

"We could still be killed, Raesh!" Carmen interrupted. "Leave her alone, she can't stop! She has to finish the spell or everybody in that portal dies! Come cast while I hold up the shield! I'll fill you in!"

Raesh huffed in frustration, but didn't say anything else. He kissed Andie on the cheek and went to help Carmen. He didn't see it, but she smiled.

Andie pushed harder, chanted louder. The fight was now being carried across the entire side of the room.

The newcomers must have numbered at least forty and more professors had come running in shortly after Raesh and Marvo arrived. The air was dangerously alive with vivid spells and shrapnel and whatever was coming out of Marvo's gun. In some places the fighters had gotten so close that it turned into a fist brawl, like the old ages. The black marble was cratered and reduced to ash and blown across the room and the air was thick with magic and dust, the sound was unimaginable. It was so loud. So unbelievably loud.

Somehow a professor got around Carmen's shield. He must have run around the outer edge to come up behind. By the time anyone saw him it was too late. He cast a viscous light into Carmen and she collapsed into a heap, the shield falling with her. He was quicker than the rest and blocked the incoming retaliation, but he opened himself up to do one more thing. He held both his hands out and sent a red beam right into Andie's side. She couldn't defend herself or stop chanting; all she could do was try to stay on her knees, despite the unbearable pain of the beam burning her side. They tried and tried to break his shield, but they couldn't and he kept fueling the beam. Finally, a spell hit his shield and decayed the light in a matter of moments, following which he took a blast from Marvo's gun and a spell from Raesh at the same time. He was torn in half.

It was Yara. She'd woken up. She came running over to Andie. She casted as she went, sending the decaying spell at several other professor's shields and leaving them vulnerable. She dropped to Andie's side.

"Someone get a shield back up!" she yelled. "Andie, how bad is it? Let me see."

Yara tugged the fabric loose from Andie's dress. Andie never let her focus fail, even to look at the wound, but she could feel the blood rolling down her side.

"I can heal this," Yara said. "Just keep doing what you're doing, Andie. You're so brave."

Yara put her hands against Andie's side and pressed in. Andie winced but didn't move. Yara began to whisper an incantation and Andie began to feel better within a matter of moments—though the wound felt large and it would likely take actual medicine to fully heal it. But Andie kept her mind on the portal; she and they continued the spell.

CHAPTER THIRTY-ONE

Andie couldn't tell which was more haunting: the screaming in the room or the screaming coming from the portal. The men and women on the mountain were reciting the incantation, but the children couldn't conquer their fear. The screams of children were terrible.

Finally, something began to happen. A tiny, gossamer connection began to manifest between herself and her people. Andie focused on it, focused every ounce of will and strength and magic on it, and tried to pull on it with the dragon essence inside of her. Now she understood what the spell was for: it was to reestablish the blood connection between herself and her people. She'd denied herself the benefit of her heritage for too long and had drifted, spiritually, from everything that made the dragonborn who they were. Even her 'natural' appearance had dimmed over the years because she hadn't allowed herself to live as she was.

Andie seized the connection, something like a supernatural thread, and began to try to reel her people back. She couldn't tell if she was summoning them or drawing them in or something else, but she knew she couldn't let go. Suddenly the pain spiked in her side and she lost focus for a split-second. The connection slipped some, but she held it. She began the incremental process again. She couldn't afford to fail now.

Her friends were fighting admirably and in fact they were proving stronger than their foes, but more professors kept coming. Andie knew that at this rate they would soon be overrun and there was only one way out of that room. But if she could get the dragonborn out, if she could set them free, they just might live to see another day.

"Andie!" Marvo shouted from somewhere behind her. "I don't know what you're doing or how much strength you have left, but your father wanted you to know something. He told me I couldn't tell you until you were ready and that I would know when that was. I think it's now. He wanted you to let go. To let go of everything: the past, what happened to your mother, your fear, your instinct to hide. He wanted you to be everything you were born to be, not what the world demanded from you. He said you couldn't be his protector or your mother's mourner or an outcast in a world that hated its own history. Let go. Embrace the power in your blood."

Her father. It had been so long since she'd seen him, but as Marvo spoke those words she could hear his voice, feel his arms. Even now, miles and circumstances apart, he was still guiding her. Still loving her. She rose to her feet, forgetting all her cares of the world and the times and the dangers of the night. In that moment, she knew only one thing: the dragon inside of her. As she tapped into that power and it exploded within her. Her hair grew and the color of it and her eyes intensified to what it was always supposed to be. Her skin took on a pearlescent sheen and the faint outlines of scales, barely noticeable, appeared on her arms. Her wounds healed in mere moments and she lifted off the ground. The thread was solid now and she reeled it in, faster and faster. She saw the end of it approach and shouted the final words of the spell, opening the portal to world.

The dragonborn poured from the portal, so many and so quickly it was impossible to count. Women, children, men, warriors, all were returning to the earth. The professors crowded together and probably would have run for the door if they were not so frightened. The newcomers smiled at the return of the dragonborn, but even they moved back. And then the real magic came. Dragons began to burst through the portal, almost too large to fit through the pool. They were incredible, colorful, powerful. Their riders were already on their backs as they circled the room.

For several brief but eternal moments, the room was frozen; newcomers, professors, monitors, Marvo, Raesh, Yara, and even Andie was frozen as they watch the dragonborn leap from the portal. Those few moments when no one moved was like a magic all its own, soundless, inert, and historic. The expressions of dragonborn were matched only by the sheer gravity of their presence. An entire race had been brought forward in time. They had very nearly been extinguished forever and yet there they stood, alive and happy and powerful. The bloodlines had become so diluted and so uncertain that it was doubtful there were many dragonborn left in the world. For all Andie knew she was the only one. But now she was surrounded by her people and by her friends, too. Andie had so many questions, so much joy, so many things to say, but she knew there would be time later. That's what the return of the dragonborn meant: time.

Suddenly, a huge wave of professors and monitors flooded the room, all of them shocked and disheartened to see the dragonborn alive again. But they weren't alone; following the monitors were the Searchers and their guns. It was clear that this was meant to be more than an attack; they were prepared to wage a small-scale war in that room and who knew how many more would come. They were right in the heart of the University.

Soon enough, the shock wore off and from somewhere in the room she heard Chancellor Myamar Mharú shout over everyone's heads.

"Kill them! Kill them all!"

"Not so fast, Mharú," said Saeryn.

"You dare speak to me? Like I was your equal?"

"You know him?" Andie asked.

"No. At least not directly," Saeryn said, gliding forward with the grace of a thousand queens and fierceness of that entire room of dragon warriors. "But the Mharú family has always hated us and they've always had those horse faces. Easily recognizable, a feature they never lost when they came over from the Old World. Of course, the name used to be Melpomene. One of the so-called great founding families."

"We are great! And we'll be even greater once we throw your corpses back into the portal. It seems you came back only to die. Fools. You could've died relatively easily by staying in there, but you came out here to our waiting hands, for a death so exacting and so brutal that even the secret histories will not be able to bear the telling of it. Such courage and stupidity you show, facing us. I sincerely hope you've said your goodbyes because I'm coming now to rip your tongue out."

"You threaten us?" Saeryn asked, perfectly calmly. "You want to test yourself against dragonborn?"

"We defeated you before."

"No, your ancestors did. Sorcerers and sorceresses much more powerful and terrifying than you. And they only succeeded because they spent decades instilling fear into the dragonborn. Decades of propaganda circulated by brilliant, if wicked, wizards who were themselves hundreds of years old. But you don't have decades. You have only minutes. If we couldn't be killed then, all those centuries ago, what makes you think you can kill us now? You're a pale approximation of the men who defeated us. Don't you know who we are? What we can do? What power we hold?"

Myamar Mharú became visibly frightened. It seemed to finally dawn on him who he was looking at and how foolish he sounded. He glanced up to see the dragons clinging to the pillars above, warriors armed with swords and no doubt trained in the most arduous and potent magic. He looked over all the dragonborn and turned pale. He didn't back down, obviously too scared of what would happen if he showed weakness, but every eye that could see him saw his fear.

"Look around you," Saeryn said, this time addressing all the professors, monitors, and Searchers. "We are not some common street nuisance. We are born of dragons. Look at our numbers, our armor, our ferocity. You would stand against us? Against all of us? And for what, so you can fulfill some age-old vendetta that even your father's father's father cannot recall? Is your hatred so strong that it has blinded you? Are you so willing to die?"

Their enemies began to look regretful, some even squeamish. Saeryn looked like a queen: beautiful, proud, and pure, as poised as the great dragons themselves.

"This one girl could dispatch you," Saeryn said, indicating Andie. "And you would pit yourselves against all our people? Think again. This may be your time, your place. But we are ancients, born of a time long past with more magic than you can know. I breathe in your diluted air and can tell that after these long centuries, even your sorcerer's magic has likewise diluted. The sorcerers nearly won in our time, nearly succeeded in eradicating us for good. We have hated and raged and feared, but now we are saved and we are strong. So now, descendants of sorcerers long past, our sworn enemy who forced us from our lands and nearly stripped us of our people, we offer you not friendship—for we could never forget those crimes of yore—but peace. Shaeyara is a vast land and there must be a place where our people can live without harm. Will you accept this offer?"

Everyone was silent. Andie watched the professors and their servants. Everyone on her side seemed to be waiting for what surely seemed inevitable: who in their right minds would challenge so many angry ancient warriors who have magic so much stronger than any we have had in our world for centuries? Dragon warriors were the fiercest fighters of ancient times and not only that, but there were dragons as well. Andie counted at least twenty and a single one would have been more than enough. Andie's allies all looked hopeful, some even lowered their hands and moved out of their stance, certain the fighting would end there. But Andie knew better; she'd lived among these people. She'd read their histories, attended their University, remembered the legends and the murals she'd seen in the secret corridors beneath them. She'd watched them drag her mother away. These people had lived in hate so long, that it had overcome them, made them numb to any other sentiment. They would never accept the dragonborn into the world again and despite their obvious apprehension, not a single one of them had lowered their hand. Not one Searcher had put away their weapon. Saeryn turned to her.

"Andryne, would you care to say anything?"

Andie paused at being called that name, but quickly held her ground and gazed fiercely out at those around her. "That won't do any good," Andie said, her feet finally on the ground again. "Look at them. All they know is destruction."

"Then what do you propose?" Saeryn asked, her hands already turning into glowing fists as she anticipated the response, the only possible answer.

Andie moved forward until she was standing

between Saeryn and Carmen. Yara, Raesh, and Marvo walked up to join the line as well. They had no misconceptions. Andie surveyed the enemy: Mharú cowering silently, Tarven hidden out of sight, professors and monitors and Searchers frightened, but determined. Andie faced Saeryn.

"Redemption. War."

CHAPTER THIRTY-TWO

I⊤ BEGAN IN A KIND OF SLOW HAZE. THE DRAGONS moved first, at the bequest of their riders, and began to soar lowly, threateningly over the enemy. The dragon warriors on the ground began to glow, unsheathing their swords as if the ancient times were not behind them but right before—a world where iron and rock still ruled the earth. The children were herded out of harm's way, but even they seemed to have some minor training in defense. The dragonborn moved like one body—men, women, old, young—driving themselves into highly coordinated ranks, impenetrable. Raesh, Marvo, and the newcomers backed up and were absorbed into the dragonborn formation. Andie, Carmen, and Yara joined the front lines. The Searchers had advanced training and formed a rather intricate phalanx designed primarily for attack. The monitors, too, engaged in a sort of crude flanking technique. The professors, who were powerful magicians but also first and foremost scholars, tried forming up, but the result was pitiable. The dragons began to move in more ferocious patterns, roaring and spitting fire at the walls; they were limited in what they could do because they were so large and had to share the space in a small corner of the room, but they were far from being set at a disadvantage.

The first spell was cast by a monitor, frightened into attack by a dragon gliding low overhead. His spell rebounded off the dragon's scales without hurting it at all. And it began.

The entire University group attacked as if they'd all been counting down the moment in their heads. The dragonborn seemed most surprised by the Searchers' guns, but even that could not intimidate them. The dragonborn shields came up like a cosmic blast of light; the enemy was still ten feet away and still they were sent back by the expulsion of wind. The dragon riders were the first to retaliate. Down they dived, spreading fire and hexes like the thickest rain, and the dragons snapped up the enemy in their great jaws and ravaged them. Some riders dismounted, dropping sword first from thirty feet in the air.

As University security, the monitors had been given two weapons. The first of these was the white fire, which could be shaped and controlled much the same as spellglass. It was a fearsome weapon and had had success against the newcomers, but the dragonborn didn't even flinch. There was no fire on earth, magical or otherwise, that could hurt them.

When the monitors saw this, they tried to use their second weapon. It was called deighilt, a very old weapon made of light and wind. The weapon was designed to tear, separate, and divide the body; it touched a person's skin and began to divide the body, first at the joints, then the waist, and finally the head. If you survived long enough to be breathing when it got to your head, you would've suffered an unimaginably painful death. It was the size of a large marble and they had pouches that contained perhaps a hundred of them. They began throwing them.

But none were so terrible and decisive as the dragonborn. They moved and fought with the honor and viciousness of another time. They struck with flashing swords and cast room-shaking spells at the same time. Their agility, strength, and instincts were flawless. They were the most lethal force Andie had ever seen. Legend told of the skill and might of the dragonborn, in war and peace times, but this was greater than all of that. They were unstoppable. Not only were they skilled on foot and on dragons, but some of the warriors could leap ten or even twenty feet in a single bound. Saeryn herself—

ever calm, ever focused—was like a nightmare or a terror in the dark, lethal and swift as a storm. Even the newcomers gave the dragonborn a wide berth.

The Searchers were the most skilled on the enemy side, by far. They could cast and shoot in rapid succession, and were highly skilled in evasion. Andie saw immediately that the cruelty of their guns had not been exaggerated: the most frightening and bloody spells shot amplified from their barrels and many newcomers fell. The professors, hardly in control of themselves now that they were full of fear, advanced behind the Searchers, casting and ducking like the cowards they were.

Raesh's devastating magic was something to behold. He cast wildly and without hesitation, furious, exacting, and strong. His father fought beside him, shooting with an aim that was a wonder all its own. Carmen and Yara fought side-by-side, more clever and more precisely than even they could believe. They erected a joint shield and cast in tandem, Yara decaying the enemy shields and Carmen whipping them with lightening and smoke. The newcomers quickly learned to fight within the dragonborn formation and the side of the allies was advancing steadily.

Andie fought like a deity. After having tapped into the magic of her blood, she became a limitless force. Her feet left the ground again and she threw spells across the enemy without mercy or restraint. She lifted them, crushed them, made ash and void of them. Following Saeryn's lead, she unleashed the purple fire of the dragons on the hooded monitors, blasting them off their feet and igniting the deighilt, which burst in their pouches and did monstrous work. Neither Andie, nor her people, relished the taking of lives, but this fight was not for individual morals or untenable peace. It was not for virtue or for honor or even for pride. It was for survival. They had to wage war and to win decisively, else-wise they would be wiped out. For good.

The fight was one-sided from the beginning and even the Searchers couldn't make way against the dragonborn. This ancient race moved with a lethal and methodological confidence. But Andie's heart broke when she heard it. His scream. She turned and saw Raesh colliding with a pillar, his chest cut from shoulder to pelvis and deep enough to see bone. She flew over to him, cascading unquenchable fire on the professor who'd cast the spell. She kneeled down beside him and took him up.

"Raesh! Raesh!"

He was unresponsive and now that she was closer, Andie could see that the wound was much worse than she'd thought. She kept shaking him and calling his name, but he wouldn't wake up. She pressed her hand on the wound and began to heal it, though it would need closer attention by someone more trained than herself.

She set him up against the pillar where he would be safe and called Marvo over.

"What's wrong?" he said.

"He's been hit and it's bad. It's really bad. I can do some superficial healing now, but he needs real medical attention. I don't know enough about healing spells."

"Listen, you can't worry about that now. This is good, you did fine. Go help your people end this. We've almost got them beat and I can watch Raesh until this is over. Go be dragonborn."

Marvo gave her an encouraging smile and Andie nodded back. She looked down at Raesh again: he'd been so brave, so fierce, so unimaginable. He'd hidden his magic for so long and then he'd gone there that night and fought with the strength of ten sorcerers. He was incredible. She kissed his cheek and shifted him over to his father. She rose and headed back to the fight.

Floating above her enemies, with her shield encompassing her completely, Andie was a force that could not be reckoned with. She was not as strong or as practiced as the rest of her people, but she was a mean opposition. She rained the fire of her ancestors down on the professors relentlessly and when they erected shields above themselves, she burned right through them.

The dragonborn were making short work of their foes and even though more forces from the University had streamed in, the fight was nearly over. At that point it had become a mere formality for the professors and

Searchers to resist; they could not have stood against the dragons or the dragonborn, and certainly not the two together. Their screams were pitiable to hear and there was a grotesque carnage where men and women once stood, but they had been offered the chance of peace and denied it.

Spells, hexes, swords, fire, deighilts, bullets, and dragons filled the air. There were screams and grunts and the dull sound of bodies collapsing on the black marble. Pillars were lifted, split, or vaporized. There was carnage and destruction like the worst nightmare. The next wave of professors and monitors ran in, saw the havoc, and immediately retreated. That was the moment everyone knew which way the battle would turn. There was a certain feel in the air as the tide turned, as centuries of bloodshed, fear, and persecution met its end. The world sat then in a new condition where might was no longer the way of the executors.

Then a dragonborn warrior was struck in the chest with something small and dark; as it hit her, it grew and tangled itself around her. It bound her arms, her neck, her head, and grew so thick she could not be seen beneath it. It was some sort of magical plant. The rider couldn't manage to stay on her dragon and she fell—it must have been close to forty feet. She fell head first and just before she hit the ground, the vines rolled back to expose her skull.

Andie would never forget the gut-wrenching sound

it made as the rider hit. The dragon reared its head in the air; it had dived to catch her but hadn't moved fast enough. It gesticulated and roared in the air, turning and coughing smoke in terrifying display of ancient fury. It opened its great jaws and Andie saw the bright glow of the flames rising from its chest. She looked to see the dragon's target. It was Tarven. He was standing stock still in his fright, a tiny ball of vines in his hand like the one that had bound the rider. The dragon's fire rose quickly. For some reason—perhaps for the good times, however false they were, or perhaps because her heart was so much purer than even she knew—Andie couldn't stop herself for reaching for him.

"Tarven, look out!"

Her scream seemed to jolt him out of his horrified stupor and he dove out of the room. Saeryn moved swift as the wind and cast a shield over all the newcomers and dragonborn, a great and luminous shield that was the strongest Andie had ever seen. The dragon's attack was unlike the small bursts it and the other dragons had used so far; this was a blast born of true hurt.

The fire filled the front of the room and then spread as far as the sides. It leapt high into the air and flooded over the shield like a flickering manifestation of death itself. Even through the shield they could feel the heat. Hundreds of cracks broke the marble as it was superheated by the flames and most the professors and Searchers lost their lives when their shields were burned away. The only reason the rest managed to survive was because they escaped the room just in time.

Andie watched in horror at the scene of burning, death, and destruction that lay in front of her. This isn't what she had wanted. This isn't what she had wanted at all.

CHAPTER THIRTY-THREE

BY THE TIME THE FIRE SETTLED DOWN, THE PROFESSORS and their bevy had escaped. Andie could hear them shouting as they ran out through the hallway and into Leabherlann. They were crazed, frightened. They were screaming at the top of their lungs, telling everyone near that the dragonborn had returned.

Saeryn exhaled in a way that Andie had not known before and not just Saeryn, but each of the dragonborn, warriors and folk alike. Even the dragons snapped shut their jaws and lay down on the floor. Strangely, without reason or logic, Andie felt it, too. The relief, the sheer ecstasy pouring into them from the undercurrents of the last centuries. Peace. Breath, life. Possibility.

Safety.

Andie also experienced the emotion of her friends and the newcomers: utter shock. For centuries, the

legends of the dragonborn had been in circulation—
mostly as bywords or cautionary tales to scare children
and delight evening parties—but never had they
understood even a piece of the majesty and power that
the forgotten race possessed. Before them stood
warriors, priests, artists, tradesmen, and children from
another time, herded from all around Shaeyara and
captured at their weakest. But now they had returned
more fearsome and shining than ever before. Andie and
her friends were shocked to see the immensity of the
dragons, the sheen of the armor, the scope and color of
the spells, and the incalculable will of these fine and
glorious people. Saeryn walked to Andie and took
her hands.

"I was not born a warrior," she began. "I was made
one through many years of hard training and
persistence. I had no natural talent or appetite for war or
the strength it required, but it was necessary. You,
however, are a born warrior. Perhaps a scholar and
priestess as well. I cannot say what single gift I see, but
there is potential in you which I have not seen since that
time from which I came. Thank you, on behalf of my
people and their families. And on behalf of our dragons.
But I also thank you for myself, for it was no mean feat
to retrieve us from such peril. I owe you the very air I
breathe."

And much to Andie's surprise, Saeryn kneeled
before her, still holding both of her hands.

"You don't need to do that," she said, nervous, flattered, and embarrassed. "I'm no queen."

"Of course not. I am."

Andie drained of color; it seemed unreal, unfair that a queen knelt to her. But before she could absorb the shock of Saeryn's gesture, the rest of her people began to kneel as well. Elderly, children, warriors, everyone bent the knee to the nervous girl who'd finally accepted herself and her place in time. The entire dragonborn race kneeled before Andie Rogers.

"It is the custom of these people to show respect to its guardians," Saeryn said. "Make no mistake, that is what you are now. I'm afraid this pales in comparison to the rites we would normally perform, but we have not the time just now. One day we will be able to repay you."

Saeryn rose and lifted her hand toward the ceiling. An enormous suction swept the room and seemed to gather all the air at once. It formed a flat, whistling vortex against the ceiling and as Saeryn flicked her fingers upward, the vortex shot up through the ceiling. Higher and higher it went, ripping and tearing marble, stone, earth, plants, and snow until it broke into the air hundreds of feet above. The hole led out somewhere on the mountainside far above. The dragon riders mounted the beautiful beasts and saluted Andie and her friends as they roared off into the giant hole on their journey to the sky. The adult dragonborn gathered the children and the elderly and ascended in crackling beams of purple light, some magic Andie had never known. She looked at Saeryn, confused.

"What's happening?"

"Andie, we must go where it's safe," Saeryn said, the space around her beginning to glow.

"But how will I find you? What will we do here? You can't leave me here. You can't leave me here alone!"

"Trust your blood and you may find us whenever you need us. Fight for who you are. Never live in shame. Together, we will prove to the world that we have every right to breathe and know peace as the rest of the lands. We are unique from sorcerers, but we need not be seen as dangerous. Merely different. We will meet again, soon, guardian. For now, we seek asylum."

And as the final word left her lips, Saeryn vanished. And with her the dragonborn were gone, again. Andie hadn't even realized that she was crying. She only wished her mother had lived to see that night.

"Everyone, to me now," Marvo called. "It's time to tell them who we are."

Marvo walked over to Andie to put his arm around her. He held her for a moment.

"Are you going to be okay?" he asked.

"Now that I know my people are alive... yeah, I'll be fine," she said, smiling.

"Good."

The newcomers gathered around Andie, Carmen, and Yara. Andie gazed around the faces and saw people she recognized: Murakami from Leabherlann, one of the working ladies from the mess hall, even the lady she'd met in the street her first night in Arvall.

"I see you found your way home after all," she said.

Andie saw professors she'd seen in the hall, a student or two, and the landlady from the restaurant—the middle-aged spinster who hadn't said a word. Kristole.

"I see you recognize a few of our faces," Marvo said. "I'm sure you remember Kristole, but what about her tattoo?"

Kristole turned around to show Andie the tattoo on the back of her neck. A hand in flames.

"Andie, cast a revealing spell on my neck," Marvo said, turning.

She waved her hand and suddenly the same hand in flame appeared on the back of Marvo's neck. She looked at it in awe. The other newcomers turned and Andie revealed the hand on all of their necks.

"Andie," Marvo said, "We're part of a secret society of allies to the dragonborn. We don't have a name, though we have from time to time been known as the Council. We're made up of outcasts; some of us are purely human, like myself, but almost all of us have sorcerer's magic, but chose to refine it by natural means rather than be brainwashed by the University. I know you've never heard of us and that's because we've stayed hidden for centuries, passing our secrets on to our children so they could be ready to fight when the time came. This is a big day for both you and us. Our ancestors fought for your people. I'm sorry that they lost, but I'm overjoyed that we succeeded. For a very long time the University led the persecution of the dragonborn and their descendants, but we've been working on that, too. From the shadows, we've gained influence and spread a desire for peace. There's a quiet, but growing push against the University and every hateful policy it seeks to uphold. Your father was at the forefront of that."

For once, Andie wasn't shocked. She knew what kind of man her father was and how much good he was capable of.

"The University found out," Marvo continued. "That's why they caused your father's accident. To corrupt his memory and take him away from the vanguard. But don't be afraid. We're going to help you and your people reunite and stand for the justice that never should have been denied you. And I can promise you one thing," he said, taking her shoulders. "You are free to be everything you always were."

Marvo hugged her and Andie looked over his shoulder to see all the encouraging and smiling faces of the newcomers. "So, this is finally it," she said quietly to herself as she pulled away from Marvo's kind embrace. "The life and the friends and the future I always wanted." Marvo let her go and Andie hurried over to Raesh. He was still unconscious, but the wound hadn't opened again. If they could get him to a doctor soon, he would be just fine.

"Stay with him while we check to make sure it's safe to leave," Marvo said, cocking his gun. "This place is full of dragon-hating sorcerers who just heard this battle echoing through the halls."

Andie nodded and took Raesh up into her arms again. Marvo and about half of the newcomers took off into the hallway and then up into Leabherlann. The rest of the newcomers combed the room looking for survivors and tending to their wounds. Carmen and Yara dropped down next to Andie. Carmen took one look at Raesh and started crying, holding her hand to his face.

"He'll be fine, Carmen, I promise," Andie said. "We just need to get him to a healer. I've done all I can for now, but a healer will fix him completely."

"He should never have been here," Carmen said through her tears. "This is all the University's fault. They'll answer for the things they've done."

"And we'll be the ones to ensure that," Yara said, reaching out to comfort Carmen and reaching the other hand out to Andie. "We won't leave you, Andie. I promise. Through fire and storm and battle, we'll stand by you."

"And I'll need you," Andie said, softly stroking

Raesh's hair. "All my people will need you. The University has no idea the hell it just brought down on itself. I think that with the right words and a little patience we can reason with the rest of Noelle. Hell, we'll reach even the farthest edges of Shaeyara. I'll go to them, just as I am, and show them that we're not dangerous or evil, and that all we want is the peace they stole for themselves. But the University must pay. We'll show them no mercy, give them no advantage. The land has had too many cycles of hate and prejudice. Now we've turned the tide."

Andie held Yara's hand, Yara held Carmen's, and Carmen touched Raesh as Andie held him. A bond was struck then and there, a pact of loyalty harder than steel. Andie looked up.

"There'll be no corner in this world where they can hide."

Made in the USA
San Bernardino, CA
13 October 2018